5/89

D1133218

# UPHILL ALL THE WAY

*Lynn Hall*

# UPHILL ALL THE WAY

Charles Scribner's Sons

NEW YORK

*Copyright © 1984 Lynn Hall*

Library of Congress Cataloging in Publication Data
Hall, Lynn.    Uphill all the way.
Summary: Seventeen-year-old Callie longs to help a
trouble-prone young man, but she finally comes to realize
some people cannot be changed.
[1. Oklahoma—Fiction]    I. Title.
PZ7.H1458Up    1984        [Fic]        83–20202
ISBN 0–684–18066–9

1 3 5 7 9 11 13 15 17 19   F/C   20 18 16 14 12 10 8 6 4 2

*Printed in the United States of America*

# 1

THE FIRST TIME I saw Truman Johnson I was sitting on the back steps with my head between my knees, recovering from surgery.

No, not mine. The surgery was the detomming of the Valdez's tomcat. But I don't think he was suffering from it any more than I was at that moment. All he had to lose was—well, what he'd already lost. My whole future was at stake. If I was going to pass out over a little cat castrating, Doc Fulcher could and would replace me, easy as scat. I could get other summer jobs, but none that paid as well or gave me the in with horse owners that this job was going to. And both the money and the in were important to my future.

Matter of fact, I'd gotten through the whole operation just fine, didn't get light-headed till it was all over and Doc was squirting Furacin powder into the incisions. Then's when I felt my face get all drained and my ears went to ringing, and Doc said, "Girl, you better go sit on the back steps till your blood comes back. Hang your head between your knees."

That was what I was doing when I heard the screen

door of Doc's house slam. It was just a little ways across the yard. I could see a pair of feet that definitely didn't belong to Doc's new wife, Yvonne. These were long old boy's feet in ratty tennis shoes with no socks.

I looked up slowly, testing my dizziness, which seemed to be letting up. Bony ankles, hairy white legs, old cutoff shorts, the longest, skinniest body I'd ever seen on man or beast, sweaty T-shirt, and then the face.

I guessed he was maybe my age or a little older. Seventeen, eighteen. The beard would have added age if it hadn't been such a failure. It was so sparse you could see chin right through it. Picture a skeleton with long, no-colored hair and an Adam's apple you could cut paper on, and you've got Truman Johnson.

But then he smiled at me and looked to me like one of those modern-art pictures of Christ suffering and forgiving.

He said, "Hi," and was shuffling toward me when the phone rang in the office and reminded me that I was the secretary of the place, starting today. I shot Truman a fast grin and got back to work.

Doc Fulcher's establishment was a converted double garage behind his house, which was on the corner of Main and Shawnee, with the house facing toward Main and the office toward Shawnee. It wasn't a bad-looking place, blue shingle with white trim to match the house and a redwood sign that said BERNARD FULCHER, DVM., LIBERTY ANIMAL CLINIC.

But on the inside—well, "clinic" was stretching it a mite, in my opinion. There was a little reception room with linoleum floors and $3.98-a-sheet paneling on the walls. There were a couple of plastic sofas, but most of

2

the room was filled with shelves of flea spray and bag balm—that's for cows—and stuff for dehorning calves.

Behind the reception room was the treatment-and-operating room, with a stainless steel table in the middle and not much room for anything else except the sink and kitcheny-looking cupboards. The whole other side of the building was storage: cases of prescription dog food, cages for patients, and a big refrigerator full of vaccines and worm caps and Olympia beer.

I'd been an employee for about three hours, but I already knew my way around pretty well. I'd been coming here for years. We had a cat that lived to be seventeen and had kidney problems almost the whole time, so I'd spent a good many Saturday mornings sitting in that front room. Not to mention all the dogs we had that got hit by cars or chewed electric cords or got into fights. My pop loves animals, but he's just not one of the lucky people of the world. The dogs all ended up in our dog cemetery in the backyard. That damned cat was the only one that kept not dying, and even Pop started wishing she would toward the end, when she was using the bathtub for a litter box.

Doc was hanging up the phone as I came in. "I got to run out to Marlin Jenson's to pull a calf," he said to me. "You hold the fort here, clean up the surgery. I'll be back around two, two-thirty. If you get any calls, you know how to get me on the truck radio?"

I nodded, hoping I could remember.

"Good girl. Yvonne'll bring you out some lunch."

He lumbered out to his pickup and drove away, leaving me watching out the front window, feasting my eyes on

3

the truck and wondering how much one like that was going for these days.

I turned around, thinking I should use this time to study up on Doc's bookkeeping system, and almost ran into Truman, the shaggy skeleton, who had apparently followed me in through the back door. We once had a dog, a mostly Irish wolfhound that somebody had dumped out along the highway. He was all bones and bristly whiskers. He came to mind suddenly.

"I guess you're my new dad's new assistant," Truman said. "I'm Truman."

"I know. I figured that out. I'm California Kiffin."

We did that dumb nodding thing you do when you're not smooth enough to shake hands. He looked me over, and I could imagine what he was thinking. She's a shrimp. Figure like barbed wire. Face like a monkey. Hair like a black Brillo pad. I stood as tall as I could, which isn't easy at my level, and looked back at him. He wasn't exactly a male model himself.

I went to the desk and started poking through the daily appointment book.

"California? Is that really your name?"

"Truman, is that really your name?" I shot back.

"I'll tell if you will." He grinned and drooped himself over the corner of the desk. At close range he had a kind of stale taco smell about him. I was half wishing he'd back off and let me get to work and half wishing I was wearing something classier than jeans and a T-shirt that said THE MORE I SEE OF MEN THE BETTER I LIKE MY DOG.

But what the heck, he was just trying to be friendly. I said, "California is my real name, and if you're planning

4

on being a friend of mine, you won't make cracks about it, okay?"

He nodded, kind of serious, and said, "Truman is mine, too. After the president, not Capote. I'm from Truman's home town. Lots of kids in Independence get named Truman. Did you know about me, that I was coming?"

"I'd heard something about it," I said, pushing back in the chair to brace my feet against the desk drawer. "There aren't many secrets in Liberty, Oklahoma, pardner. So if you've got a checkered past, forget about trying to hide it."

I was only kidding when I said that, but from the look on his face I figured I must have hit the old nail right on the thumb. Actually, all I knew about him was that he was the son of Doc Fulcher's new wife, Yvonne, and that he'd stayed behind in Kansas City to finish out the school year. Doc had been a bachelor for as far back as I could remember. People said he was too darn tight to get married. But for some reason that no one in town had figured out yet, he latched onto Yvonne Johnson, who had come down from Kansas City last fall to take care of her dying mother or father, I forget which.

Now, Yvonne is probably a very nice lady and all that, kind of little and birdy and quiet. But she's got false teeth that don't fit right, so they click when she talks, and she's always got little bubbles at the corners of her mouth. And you don't want to stand too close when she talks, because she sprays a lot on the *s* words. First time I met her I figured there was hope for me yet. If she could find two men to marry her. . . .

I ain't no Shirley Temple, folks, but at least I talk dry.

5

Truman was still hanging around a while later when Yvonne brought me out my lunch. It was a little dish of watery canned chicken noodle soup and two crackers, not enough to make a dent in my belly-growls. But I smiled and thanked her. This job was too important to risk getting the boss's wife mad at me.

I saw the look she gave Truman. It seemed to me she was wondering how much he'd told me about family secrets, maybe warning him to keep a zipped lip. She told him his lunch was ready in the house, so he followed her out, but in a few minutes he was back. His lunch apparently hadn't been any more sumptuous than mine.

We'd already covered the stock questions like what year are you in in school—I was going to be a senior, he had just graduated—and he'd already told me he didn't have any immediate plans for the future, he was going to take a little time off this summer to decide what he wanted to do.

Finally he got around to asking me what I planned on doing after high school. I could tell he was expecting some dull answer, like get married. So I enjoyed shooting the facts to him.

"I'm going to be a farrier."

I loved it when he did that little double take.

"A what?"

"Farrier. You know. A horseshoer."

"You can't do that, that's a man's job."

Somehow I knew he was going to say that.

"It's a woman's job, too, now."

"But you have to be strong, don't you?"

6

"I'll only have to pick up their feet," I snapped, "not the whole horse."

"But you're so short," he argued.

I shook my head. "That's to my advantage. I won't have to bend over so far."

He looked doubtful, so I went on. This was a subject I could always talk on, and I'd already worn out my family and friends. "Look, it's a good career. All I'll have to have is a three-month course at a farriery school, a pickup truck to work out of, and about seven or eight hundred dollars' worth of equipment and shoe stock, and I'll be set for life. Those guys make thirty bucks for a shoeing, and the shoes cost maybe three, four dollars. All the rest is profit. You do five or six horses in a day, and that's good money. I could spend four years in college and come out with, say, a teacher's degree that wouldn't earn me anywhere like the money I'd be making with my own farrier business, and I might not be able to get a job at all. And I'd be trapped inside all day, every day. This way I'll be my own self-employed boss within three months after high school."

I couldn't help grinning. I'd had this farrier idea for the better part of a year now, and it still excited me just thinking about it.

"Well, all's I've got to say," Truman said as he moved toward the door, "nobody's ever going to want to marry a woman who makes her living shoeing horses."

"That's their tough luck," I yelled after him. I shook my head and waved him away, and went back to trying to figure out the bookkeeping.

\* \* \*

7

I jogged home through the shortcut between houses and across yards. That way it was just a block and a half. People in Liberty don't mind if kids cut across their yards since nobody has much grass anyhow, mostly just dust.

The Egglestons were having supper on their back porch as I jogged past. Mrs. Eggleston yelled, "How did it go, Cal?"

I slowed and jogged backward to answer. "Not too bad. At least he didn't fire me yet. I didn't throw up during surgery," I crowed.

The jogging was part of my muscle-building program. Along with saving money for farriery school and my truck and going along with Don Baker to watch how he does stuff, I'm also preparing for my future career by getting physically fit.

Through Egglestons' and McCoys' yards I jogged across Temple Street, up the empty house's driveway, across the alley, and into my own backyard where five wooden crosses mark the dogs' graves. For some reason the cat didn't get a marker. I think we were all just flat-out relieved when old Boots finally bought the farm. There wasn't much mourning over that one.

Pop was watching for me out the kitchen window, the way I knew he would be. When he saw me coming, his head disappeared. Going to put supper on the table, I hoped. That watery little old bit of soup had quit holding me up three hours ago.

Pop and I have two ways of moving around the house, quiet for when Mom is asleep and relaxed for when she's at work. She's a dietitian in the hospital in Fort Supply, which is a thirty-mile drive, and she works three to eleven, then stays awake all night and sleeps all day till two, which means I haven't seen her since maybe February or March. I'd hate to tell you how little I miss her, for fear you'd get the wrong idea. She and I get along fine. Of course, the fact that we never see each other might have something to do with that.

I jogged into the kitchen and slowed to a halt, still running in place but slowing gradually to let my pulse ease off.

"Well?" Pop said. Good old Pop, already dishing up the beef stew and dumplings. It was his best dish. Knowing Pop, I figured he'd planned it that way, either to celebrate my first day on the job, or to cheer me up if it had been a disaster.

You'd like my Pop. He looks kind of like a leprechaun, and everyone in town calls him Pop. He's not a whole lot taller than me, kind of a leathery little guy but with the sweetest face. People are always saying how much I look like him, which is weird under the circumstances. I don't think I want to tell you what the circumstances are, though. Maybe later.

"I survived," I told him, jogging to a stop. The bathroom is right off the kitchen, so I could talk while I washed up. "It was even fun. I helped with an operation, castrating Valdez's cat, and I cleaned up after it, and Doc was gone most of the afternoon so I took phone calls and learned where stuff was, and like that. Man, that smells good."

9

I sat down and started shoveling stew. "One bad thing: the lunches over there aren't exactly going to be gut busters. I think I'll start taking sandwiches."

After I'd told him every detail of my day he said, "Well, good. It sounds like it's going to work out okay for you for the summer. I was kinda holding my breath all day. Doc's always been pleasant enough to me, but then, I'm a paying customer. I didn't know how he'd treat help. Did you get a look at his new son?"

I snorted.

"What's he like?"

I shrugged.

"You don't sound overly impressed," Pop said with that twinkle he gets in his voice.

"Not overly. He didn't even know what a farrier was."

"City kid, I expect."

"I don't know." I frowned. "Now that I think about it, we talked a long time today and he never said two words about where he'd lived or his old school or anything. We mostly talked about me."

That's another one of my faults, talking about myself too much. I'll work on it.

Pop said Carol didn't need me tonight, so I washed the dishes and cleaned up the kitchen while he got ready to go to work. Carol was his boss and sometimes mine. Pop worked part time at the movie theater, sweeping up five mornings a week and runing the projector three or four nights. Carol was the theater manager, when she felt like it. About half the time she hired me to sell tickets and refreshments while she went out with some jerk, usually of the traveling salesman variety. Her love life was in a slump at the moment, so I wasn't getting much evening work.

But that was okay. I was ready to flop for a while. First day on a new job takes it out of you, even if the work isn't all that hard. It's the strain of learning all that new stuff, like working the microphone on the desk to call Doc on his truck radio and tell him about the calls that had come in, and how to work the autoclave to sterilize all those surgical gizmos.

So after supper I turned on the TV and went out to the front porch where, if you angle it right, you can lie in the hammock, watch the TV through the window with your left eye, and keep track of the neighborhood with your right eye.

My muscles were just easing loose when Don Baker's pickup cruised up and honked. He waved and I waved and went down across the yard to see what he had to say. Don Baker's truck is my dream. It's a dark-green Dodge one-ton with a white fiberglass shell on the back and signs on the doors that say, DON BAKER, HORSESHOEING, LIBERTY, OKLA.

He's a handsome dude, more Mexican than not, teeth you can see a mile away. He said, "I'm going out to Hensels' to trim up a couple of colts. Want to come?"

I went. I'm never too tired to go help Don.

The Hensel place was nothing fancy, but they did have about twenty head of good quarter horses and they took fine care of them. It was one of the places I coveted for my own business a year or two down the road. Of course that coveting ignored the problem of Don. I liked him too much to want to take customers away from him.

11

Mr. Hensel was waiting for us with two sorrel yearlings tied to the fence. I talked to him and the colts while Don tied himself into his leather apron and clanked around in his toolbox for his nippers and rasp. When he was ready, I held the first colt by the halter and scratched his neck to get his mind off what Don was doing to him.

That first colt did a lot of dancing and bobbing around on three legs fighting Don, till Don finally whammed him in the side with his fist and made him settle down. I tried to watch exactly what Don was doing, but most of the time I couldn't see over his shoulder. The second colt was much quieter though, and after Don had done the front hoof, he offered me the second one.

I looked at Mr. Hensel, who nodded. My hands were shaky but I didn't let on. I just crouched over that hoof and tucked it up tight between my knees and held out my hand for the hoof knife. Carefully I pared away the dirt that was packed up into the concave sole.

Don took the knife away and handed me the nippers. "Take the wall off even with the sole all the way around."

I gritted my teeth and clamped those nippers around that hoof wall and squeezed. They bit through. Glorious feeling. I inched them along and bit again and again all the way around the hoof until there was a crescent of excess hoof peeling up from the nippers. Don gave me the rasp, and I tried to file the hoof down smooth, but it's almost impossible without leather gloves and apron. You end up filing your own legs. So Don took over and finished up.

I grinned all the way home.

We went back to his house and sat around the kitchen table with his wife, Juanita, who'd been two years ahead of me in school. It was her brother's cat that Doc and I had operated on that morning, so she had to hear all about that. We propped our feet up on each other's chair rungs and drank Dr. Peppers and ate Doritos from a bag in the middle of the table. Juanita was extremely pregnant then and couldn't seem to get comfortable in any position.

Sometimes I got a little irritated with Juanita. She was always just as nice as pie to me, even while she was pregnant. It was a little insulting. I'd just been out riding around the countryside with her husband, and I was working up toward being his competition in business. It didn't seem to me that she was considering me much of a threat on either of those fronts.

I thought she might show a little nastiness when Don told her I'd trimmed a hoof, but she just grinned and made a face when the baby kicked her.

"You ought to pay Cal an eighth of your fee, then," she said to Don.

I said, "I'm taking it in Doritos."

"So did you meet Yvonne's son?" she said. "I heard he got here yesterday. Maybe that'll be a little love interest for you to brighten your working day, huh?"

I snorted. "No chance. They've got to at least have half a brain, or I'm not interested. And he's too skinny and too tall, and he's trying to grow this stupid beard because he doesn't have any chin, but the beard is so scrawny you can see right through it." I hunched my shoulders just thinking about it.

13

"Is he in school?" Juanita asked, shifting in her chair.

"Just graduated, I guess. I couldn't get him to tell me much about himself."

Don reached for the Dorito bag and said, "From what I heard about him, I don't think that was a high school he just graduated from, kiddo. More like a county jail or reform school or some such."

I stared at him. "You're kidding."

"That's what I heard."

I stopped crunching to ponder. I'd never known a criminal before. Interesting.

"I'll ask him about it tomorrow," I said.

# 2

"GET A GOOD GRIP on his lip, now. Here we go."
Doc's voice was cheerful. Hell, why shouldn't he be cheerful? He wasn't the one hanging on a seventeen-hand
stallion by a lead rope and a twitch on his lip.

The stallion was cross-tied in the aisle of the brown-and-white-polka-dotted barn at Happy Appy Acres, and
at this moment he was not a happy Appy, nohow. There
I was, working the big steel clamp that held the horse's
lip and theoretically took his mind off of whatever else
was being done to him that was more unpleasant than
having his lip twitched and talking to him in my best
horse-soothing tone. And there was his owner, standing
way out of firing range of those big, steel-shod hooves. And
there was Doc, coming at him with five feet of rubber hose
and a balling gun. Now this horse was no fool. He knew
something rotten was coming, and he wasn't about to
surrender without a fight.

Doc laid a hand on the stallion's face and started slipping
the end of the hose up a nostril. The horse screamed and
flung himself up in the air. The twitch went flying. I
grabbed the lead rope with both hands as he jerked me

15

into the air. A hoof knocked me in the hip, but we landed okay, since the cross-tie ropes kept him from going up very high. He bounced and snorted a couple more times and took a swipe at me with his teeth. Missed.

"You okay?" Doc asked from the sidelines. He didn't sound especially worried.

"Yeah," I muttered, just about equally mad at Doc and at the stallion.

We went at it again, and after another eight or ten minutes of hassling, Doc finally got the tube all the way up that devil's head, down his throat, and into his stomach. He shot the worming medicine home, then whipped the hose out of the horse with a theatrical sweep, and handed all the gunky stuff to me to wash up while he went outside to have a smoke with the owner.

We tube-wormed the whole stable: stallion, six mares with foals at their sides, four yearlings, and a two-year-old. Most of them fought us in one way or another. The temperature was up around a hundred and not a breath of air moving anywhere, and I'll tell you, along about mid-afternoon death was beginning to look like a pleasant alternative.

But the whole time I was working I was watching myself, too, testing how I was holding up under it, because I was going to have plenty of days like this in the future, rassling horses that didn't want their feet messed with, just like these didn't want that tube up their noses. I needed to find out if I could take it, and when that last colt was led away and Doc and I were sterilizing the equipment and loading it into the truck, I had a feeling of such power and victory, like nothing I'd felt before in my

16

life. It made me feel sorry for the girls I knew who were aiming at easy stuff, like secretary jobs.

I collapsed in the truck seat and closed my eyes, but I could feel Doc looking at me.

"You okay?"

I nodded. "Just pooped. Bruised hip from when that stallion got me. Nothing serious."

I opened my eyes and glanced at Doc. He didn't look used up at all. But then, he'd had rests between each horse and a considerable amount of cold beer with the owner while the stable hands and I were setting things up and catching the next victim.

"How much money did we just make, Doc?" I asked idly.

"I made a couple hundred bucks. You made two-fifty an hour."

I gave him a dirty look. We'd been working together all week now, and I felt confident enough for an occasional dirty look. Doc Fulcher brought a pig to mind, just the way Truman brought to mind our old half-starved Irish wolfhound. Doc's face wasn't really fat, but he had pounds of jowls hanging and swinging there and little greedy eyes and a pug nose that turned up just enough so you had the feeling of looking up his nostrils. Of course I have that feeling with lots of people, being as short as I am. Nose hair is nothing new to this kid.

Gradually I was beginning to realize that it wasn't just the way Doc looked that reminded me of pigs. It was all the little things, like the lunches that were supposed to be part of my pay: small bowl of watery soup every day, three crackers maximum. Doc knew I was bringing sand-

17

wiches and eating them with the soup, but he ignored the hint.

And I was beginning to notice that all the unpleasant jobs, like helping with all those tube-wormings today, were given to me as though he was Santa Claus. Good experience for a future farrier. Uh-uh. Tell me how holding a furious, half-wild barn cat for a rabies shot is going to help me shoe horses.

At least I was beginning to relax about one thing— Truman. He'd been hanging around all week, more or less helping out. Today he was watching the phone while Doc and I wormed horses. Yesterday he'd gone out with Doc to castrate some calves while I held down the fort. It occurred to me that Truman was doing pretty much the same things Doc was paying me for and doing them free, and it also occurred to me that Doc wasn't one to pay for what he didn't have to. I had begun to see my dream job slipping into Truman's hands.

But by now I could see that I had one huge advantage over Truman. I was Doc's bonded servant, bought and paid for, while Truman could—and usually did—wander away if the job got hard or boring.

All week I'd been wanting to get Truman alone so I could ask him about his evil past, but Doc was always there or clients or Yvonne or somebody. I kept looking at Truman to see if I could see anything criminal or jail-birdy about him, but he looked just like the guys at school —at least the sleazier guys.

When we got back to the office, Truman was there, reading a comic book with his feet up on my desk. It was after closing time so I didn't bother to run him off my

18

territory. I just got my lunch bag and the book I was reading out of the typewriter well and started to leave. I'm not one of the great daily bath-takers of the world, but I was having fantasies about soaking in the tub while Pop put supper on and then not moving again till morning.

But Truman had a surprise for me. He followed me out the back door and said, "You want to go out after a while? Drive around or something?"

My first reaction was to look around to see if he was talking to someone else. My second was to think, no, I'd rather loaf around home. But my third was to say okay, which I did.

I don't know whether I should admit this or not, but I am not what you could call an early bloomer socially. Here I was, seventeen, and I'd never actually been out with a guy—just Don when he took me along on jobs, and a couple of times when Shelly and I drove over to Fort Supply to pick up my mom after work and picked up guys first. But even then I was always the one that the loser got. You know, you meet a couple of guys and decide to go riding around together, and then the guys go into a huddle to decide who gets who, and the one who comes up smiling always lands in the back seat with Shelly, while the loser gets me.

So I told Truman okay, and I was even a little excited about it going home, although Truman was way below what I considered my level. Don Baker—now he was my level, if Juanita hadn't beat me to him. But at least Truman was a date. Kind of.

I should probably tell you who Shelly is. Shelly Riley. She's my best friend, but she takes off every summer with her family, for a job that used to make me sick with jealousy before I got a better job with Doc. Shelly's mom is a kindergarten teacher and her dad has a little plumbing business, but in the summertime they are carny. That's the way Shelly says it: "They are carny." That means they have this trailer thing that folds out into a carnival game. You throw darts at balloons and win incredibly junky prizes. Anyway, the three of them take off as soon as school is out and travel all over the Southwest with this carnival. According to Shelly they make a ton of money and have a ball, but then Shelly's so stuck up she'd never admit that anything she did or had wasn't better than anybody else's.

She used to drive me nuts promising to take me along the next summer and then the next summer and the next, but nothing ever came of it. She just enjoyed torturing me. This was the first year I didn't want to go, and I think she was a little ticked off.

Shelly has this wild, frizzy red hair that stands out almost to her shoulders and a body that would make you sick, at least if you had a shape like mine. But then, I keep telling myself, a big chest would only get in a farrier's way. On a carny barker it's probably an asset.

I jogged home, concentrating on not limping on the hurt hip side in case any nosy neighbors reported it to Pop. If he thought I was doing anything dangerous working for Doc, that would be the end of the job. And the way everybody in this town loved my pop, things got reported back to him. Like Shell and me picking up guys in Fort Supply.

20

Or even worse, somebody went to Pop once and told him that Mom was sitting around in taverns all night after she got off her shift. Well, she was, I guess, but only with a couple of nurses who worked the same shift. They weren't doing anything wrong, and Pop didn't care, but I think it hurt him a lot that people were talking about it behind his back and feeling sorry for him. I finally told Mom she ought to have more consideration for him. After that she started going to one of the nurses' apartments and they'd play cards all night, so it worked out okay, but I never quite forgave her for not thinking of it herself. I shouldn't have had to tell her to be gentle with Pop's feelings.

When I told Pop I was going out with Truman he looked undecided, between worried and glad his doggy daughter finally managed to hook a date. I told him we wouldn't go out of town, and I'd probably be home before he was. He said we should come on down to the theater and watch the show from the projection booth. I left it open.

I stewed around a long time trying to decide what to wear. On the one hand I wanted to surprise Truman with how beautiful and feminine I was after hours, and on the other hand I was scared of overdoing it, making the evening a big deal when he probably wasn't thinking of it that way. And to tell you the truth, I never have felt right in anything but jeans. Get a skirt on me and I feel like a female impersonator at one of those weirdo clubs in Tulsa.

I settled for a denim prairie skirt and a kind of a peasant blouse and no hose or makeup. Even at that, as

21

soon as I saw Truman lounging against Yvonne's car door in the same dirty grubbies he'd been sweating in all day, I knew I was overdressed.

For a while we drove around saying things like, "What do you want to do?" "I don't care. What do you want to do?" Finally, in desperation, I suggested Pop's projection booth, and Truman jumped at the idea. I think it was the getting in free part that got to him.

We went up the stairs between the theater and the Salvation Army store, then in the door at the first landing. The projection room was long and dark, lighted mostly by the beam that came from the projector. There are two projection machines, one that's on and a second one that's threaded up and ready to go, so when you come to the end of the reel, you can switch to the other machine so smoothly nobody in the audience knows about it. The machines are taller than me—but then what isn't?—and bolted to the oily plank floor. Back in the corner there's a little workbench for splicing film and a big chair up on a platform, where the projectionist can sit and watch the movie and keep an eye peeled for the little mark in the corner of the picture that flashes when it's time to change machines.

Pop and Truman got engrossed in the machinery, Pop explaining and Truman pretending he was smart enough to follow. I climbed up in the chair and watched the movie and thought about the joys of dating.

But later on the evening got better. We went to the Chicken Inn and sat in the car and ate barbecues and hush puppies, and we talked. Finally.

Not being one to mince words, I said, "I hear you used to be in jail before you moved down here."

His adam's apple did a couple of yo-yos, but he said, "Nah. Tumbleweed Ranch. Jail would've been easier."

"What's Tumbleweed Ranch?" I wasn't sure I was going to believe him.

"It's this place up there. A working cattle ranch, for boys from broken homes or kids that their parents can't handle. I got caught selling a little grass on the school grounds, so they put me on probation and sent me to Tumbleweed for my senior year."

I looked at him over my Coke cup. "You got out for good behavior, did you?"

"I got out for being eighteen. I'm on my own now, supposedly."

"What kind of place was it, the ranch?"

"It was hell. They had this theory that hard work and fresh air were going to straighten us out, see. And then, in between the schoolwork and the livestock chores and the post-hole digging and bunkhouse building and everything else they could think of to make us do, they'd slip in all this . . . understanding." He screwed up his face and shuddered. "Do you have any idea how terrible it is to have somebody all the time telling you they understand?" he demanded. "And then they'd bring in all the religion junk, and the social workers who would try to buddy up to you so they could understand you some more. Hell, they didn't want to understand me. They wanted to straighten me out, which means making me over into their idea of what I was supposed to be."

23

"So did they? Did they improve you any at all?"

He sniffed and looked sideways down at me. "You know the one thing that place taught me? They taught me what I want out of life."

I sat up. Now we were getting somewhere—confessions of the soul and sharing serious thoughts and all that.

"What's that?"

"What I want out of life," he said, "is to get through life without ever doing a lick of work." He grinned down at me as though he'd said something brilliant.

"That's stupid, Truman. Nobody gets through life without working, unless they're rich, which you obviously aren't. How do you think you're going to earn a living?"

He shrugged. "What do I need a living for? Doc's feeding me, Ma's taking care of me. I can use her car whenever I want. Why should I bust my butt working some stupid job?"

His denseness made me speechless. I sputtered a while before I came out with, "But that can't last forever. Doc is as tight as the vest on a statue, Truman, in case you hadn't noticed. He's not going to let you mooch off him very long. You've got to have money, sometime."

"Maybe. But you don't have to work for it." He shot me an evil grin.

"What are the alternatives?" I said suspiciously.

He just shrugged.

"You going to go back to selling drugs? That's not a very intelligent goal in life, Truman."

He shrugged again. "Probably not. You have to have connections for that, and I don't know anyone down here. Besides, this town is too small for that business."

24

"Well, I'm certainly glad to hear that."

"What do you care?" He sounded curious.

"Well, I don't know that I really *care*, Truman. I mean, I'm not madly in love with you or anything, but you are a friend and I hate to see you . . . not wanting to do something with your life. Like, take me for example. The best thing in my life is my plan for the future. I'm really excited about my farrier career. I'm saving every penny I can get toward my truck. I'm working out to build up my muscles, reading books on the psychology of horses and how to handle them. I'm even sending away for brochures from different farriery schools already. It's my dream."

He looked at me as though he was trying to figure out if I was on the level. "You really mean it, don't you?"

I nodded. I was afraid to say anything more for fear of sounding like a social worker.

"I never thought about it that way. You know, Cal, you might just turn out to be a good influence on me. You want the job of straightening me out?"

Flatly I said, "I wouldn't touch it with a vaccinated crowbar."

We laughed and talked a while more, with a friendly feeling growing between us little by little. Driving home, I wondered if he was going to try anything and more than half hoped he wouldn't. Already I was beginning to see myself as a kind of saint in his opinion. Well, not saint, but Woman Full of Earth-Love and Wisdom, to be looked up to. I figured if he could rassle me down on the car seat, it would dent the image.

But on the other hand, when he just coasted the car up to the curb and waited for me to jump out and then drove off as fast as he did, I wasn't crazy about that either. It didn't say much for old Cal Kiffin in the sex-appeal department.

He probably respected me too much, I said to myself. Self, I said, he respects you too much to make a cheap pass.

But I wasn't buying that. I couldn't see Truman having that much respect for anyone or anything.

Pop wasn't home yet. I tried going to bed, but it was too hot to sleep so I sprawled on the living-room floor in the dark in front of the window fan and watched the Friday Night Creature Feature. It was about something slimy out on the desert that took over people's minds. I get a charge out of those stupid things, except I had trouble following this one because I kept thinking about Truman and wondering if it was possible to be a good influence on somebody whose idea of a good life is never having to do a lick of work.

I had my doubts.

But on the other hand, I'd always loved a challenge. No guts, no glory. Right?

# 3

"THAT'S IT. LOCK the doors," Doc said as Mrs. Mueller left carrying her collie puppy toward the car.

It was Saturday noon. Saturday morning was small animal time, and then the office closed at noon so Doc could watch his ball games on TV. I figured there would be no free lunch today. Thank God.

Truman had been hanging around the reception room most of the morning, getting in my road and making comments about my typing. Doc said rabies certificates should be typed. I didn't take typing in school, figuring I wouldn't need it in my farriery business, so it was taking me considerably longer to type the certificates than it was taking Doc to shoot the shots.

He laid Mrs. Mueller's card in front of me but said, "Leave it till Monday. That's to be billed to the breeder, by the way, not to Mrs. Mueller."

I glanced at the card and did a double take. The woman had come in to have her new puppy checked over, just to be sure he didn't need anything. The total charges were over eighty dollars.

"No wonder she looked mad when she left," I said.

27

"You really found eighty dollars worth of stuff wrong with that puppy? He looked fine to me."

Doc grinned and fished an Olympia out of the refrigerator. I noticed he didn't offer one to me or Truman.

"Tricks of the trade, my dear," he said, popping the tab and smiling down at me. He'd started calling me his dear the last day or so. It made my skin creep.

"What do you mean by that, tricks of the trade? You mean he didn't need all that stuff?" I glanced at the card again. Dewclaw removal, thirty dollars. Heartworm test, fifteen. Worming, eighteen. DHL and parvo booster shots, twenty.

"Aw, come on, Doc, who do you think you're kidding with all this stuff?" I followed him back into the treatment room where he was, for once, cleaning up after himself. Our family had had enough dogs in my time; I could tell a padded bill when I saw one.

"As I said, my dear, tricks of the trade. Sure she was mad when she left, but not at me, see? She was mad at the breeder who sold her a puppy that needed eighty dollars worth of treatment. It's the breeder who has to pay the bill, and the breeder lives in Fort Worth. The breeder's not my client, so I'm not risking losing a client by sticking it to him. See what I mean?"

"But this, but that puppy didn't . . ." I spluttered. "Look, dewclaw removal. There's no reason to remove the dewclaws, not on a collie. And a four-month-old puppy is too young for a heartworm test. And he'd already had his shots and worming before he left the breeder's. Mrs. Mueller showed me his health record when she brought him in."

28

"That's true, my little simpleton, but I'm eighty dollars richer than I would have been if I'd told her that, now aren't I? Listen, it's common practice. Don't look so shocked. I'll tell you the best one I ever heard. This friend of mine up in Colorado had this client that came in with a brand-new standard poodle she'd paid a couple of thousand dollars for. He told her the dog needed a seven-hundred-dollar eardrum transplant. Told her the ears had been infected so long the drums were covered with scar tissue and the dog would go deaf without a transplant. And the woman bought it. Course, it was the breeder that had to pay, but she was out east someplace and couldn't very well fight it long distance."

I stared. "You mean he actually did an eardrum transplant? I didn't know there was such an operation."

"There isn't," Doc said placidly. "He just kept the dog a few days and sent it home good as new. Dog never went deaf, the owner couldn't see into his head to see if there were surgery scars, everybody lived happily ever after."

"Except the poor breeder out east who got stuck with a seven-hundred-dollar rip-off," I flared.

"Don't bite the hand that's paying your salary, smart mouth."

I backed off, but I readjusted my opinion of Doc and the veterinary profession by a few notches. Downward.

Truman, who had been listening to all this while pretending not to, said, "Say, Dad, with all this money you've been raking in here this morning, how's about floating me a loan so I can take my best girl out. It's gonna be Saturday night here pretty soon."

He threw me a look that probably would have been a

wink if he'd had the coordination. I took that to mean I was his best girl and he was planning to take me out tonight. News to me, on both counts.

But Doc tossed his empty beer can and said, "Forget it, kid. Nobody gets anything for nothing in this life. You might as well learn that now. What you get, you have to work for, like the rest of us. Oh, Cal, make a note for ten o'clock Monday morning, surgery for the Mueller puppy. Got to close an umbilical hernia."

"You mean one of those teeny little hernias that most collie puppies have and that don't need to be closed? You couldn't sell her an eardrum transplant, huh?"

"Just make the appointment."

I noticed he didn't call me his dear.

After Doc left I said to Truman, "Were you asking me out for tonight, or what?"

"I was, but I'm too broke now. Unless you want to go up and watch the movie from the projection booth again. It's a different show tonight."

A truly heartwarming invitation.

"Listen, Truman, I know this sounds like a radical suggestion, but has it occurred to you to get a job?" I was fast losing all my fondness for this family. Last night's rosy dreams about saving this soul from himself were stretching thin. Of course that was probably just disgust at Doc. I shouldn't let it get in the way of helping Truman.

He shrugged his thin, hunched shoulders and said, "The thing of it is, I don't know anybody in town. Nobody knows me, except what they've heard about me being at Tumbleweed Ranch. Who's going to take a chance hiring me when they could get some local guy?"

30

Hope was reborn in my indomitable soul. "You mean you'd get a job if you had the chance?"

"I guess so. Yeah, sure."

"Okay. I'll help you. What kind of job do you want, and I'll see if I can find somebody who knows somebody."

His face went blank. Obviously it was a tough question. "What kind of job?"

"Yeah. You know, bank president, construction crew, gas station—what do you want to do?"

"I don't know," he said stupidly. "I never gave it much thought."

"I can tell. So think about it now. Do you have any experience at all, of any kind?"

He looked mildly trapped. "No, just ranch work, at Tumbleweed. But I didn't like it much. You had to be outside all the time, in the hot sun."

I sighed. "Okay. I'll ask around and see what I can come up with."

I was most of the way home before I realized I didn't know if we had a date tonight or not. Well, I figured I'd find out when he showed up or didn't.

Mom was in the kitchen when I got home. She was sitting in her bathrobe, staring at nothing and stirring a cup of coffee. Breakfast time for her, lunchtime for me. I avoided her space and went to work on a fat sandwich as quietly as I could. On weekends Mom always seemed to be in a bad mood. My theory is that she missed going to work. That was where she really lived.

She used to be pretty. Most of it's still left, but it's getting thicker and baggier. She's got long, dark hair and blue eyes and nice, kind of pinkish skin. She likes to brag about being pure English, about her English complexion. She's not a happy person, so I know I'm supposed to feel sorry for her and be understanding and all that. But it's uphill work when you really don't understand. I can't see that she has anything to bitch about. She couldn't have a more loving, adoring husband than Pop, and I'm not such a bad kid. I never get into trouble and I'm going to be self-supporting in record time practically, without even costing them college money. She loves her job, and she pretty much does whatever she wants.

So I have to wonder if she's not unhappy because she likes it that way. I keep having this feeling she's punishing Pop for something, even though it should be the other way around.

I guess I can tell you. It's no big deal anyway. I'm sure the world is full of kids who don't know who their real father is. And when you've got a Pop like mine you'd be crazy, not to mention ungrateful, to get in a sweat worrying about who actually supplied the other half of the genes.

Neither one of them ever told me about it, but in a house the size of ours you can learn as much as you want just by moving quietly. She was pregnant when Pop married her, and she never would tell him who the man was. Figuring their ages and mine, she would have been about twenty-two and he about forty when they got married. Why he did it, who knows? Except it's not all that surprising when you know Pop. Anything he can do for anybody, any time, he's right there with the offer.

What I've never been able to figure out, though, is how come she hates him? He did her a real favor. In a town like this, even now, it's awful hard on girls who get pregnant. Way back then it would have been worse. The way it worked out, with me even looking like Pop, everyone just assumes they got a little previous, and Pop did the right thing and married her. That's acceptable. But if he hadn't, she would have been in for a rough time of it. So how come she's not grateful?

After my stand-up lunch I followed Mom's muttered directions and found Pop on a ladder at Ada Hendrikson's, three houses down the street. Ada was a widow, sort of a professional leaner if you ask me. She was a sweet little old lady, but I don't think she'd ever done a thing for herself if she could possibly get her son or my pop to do it for her. Pop loved her.

He was up near the peak of her house's roof, painting the trim. It was a one-story house, so he was low enough to talk to. I sat down on the ground, out of range of his paint, although he was a very neat painter. I'd no sooner got sat when I was pounced on by a pup I'd never met before. He was maybe half-grown, in that loose, soft stage where you just want to hug them all the time. He looked like mainly dachshund. He wove through my legs and snaked up to lick my chin.

"Who's this?" I called up to Pop.

"That's our new dog. Adolf. Ada's son dumped him on her to get rid of. I guess they got him for the kids, but he wasn't getting housebroken fast enough to suit the wife. I told her we'd take him and the kids can have visiting privileges. He seems like a nice little guy, huh?"

"Yeah, Pop." Well, we were about due. Our last dog ran away three, four months ago.

33

"Listen, Callie, you can take him to work with you Monday morning and have Doc look him over, okay? See if he needs shots or worming or anything."

"I wouldn't do that if I were you," I muttered, and told him about the morning's revelations regarding the good doctor.

Pop just laughed. "That man is so tight, he breathes through his nose to save wear and tear on his teeth."

"Pop, this goes beyond tight. It's downright dishonest, telling people their dogs need things they don't really need."

"Caveat emptor."

"What's that mean?"

"Means buyer, beware. People ought not to be so trusting, I reckon. But we always are with professional people, doctors, lawyers, vets. Still, I don't think Doc would cheat us. You take Adolf over there Monday, okay?"

I gave up. He'd never believe anything bad about anybody.

I rolled Adolf around on the ground awhile and tried throwing a stick for him, but he didn't know that game.

"Pop?"

"Mmm."

"Can you think of anybody offhand that would maybe give Truman a job?"

"What kind of job? What can he do?"

I laughed. Not kindly.

"Okay then," Pop said, "what could he learn?"

I rubbed Adolf's chest, which he was offering up. "Some kind of ranch-hand job maybe, I don't know. Something that didn't take too many smarts."

34

He pondered, then lowered himself for a refill from the paint can. "You could always ask John Gray, I reckon. He knows more people and hires more people than anyone I can think of in town here. But I'd want to be sure of the person I was getting the job for before I went and bothered John about it. You know, like would Truman be a good employee and all that. You wouldn't want to ask favors of somebody like John unless you were sure you were sending him somebody he'd want to have working for him. Truman honest, is he?"

I thought a long time over that one and finally said, "He's as lazy as three old cats, but I don't quite see him stealing, or that sort of thing. He got in trouble once for selling marijuana at school, but he's not doing that anymore."

He hunkered down beside me and looked worried. "I don't know, darlin'. Your friend Truman doesn't just exactly fill me with trust and confidence. How's come you to be looking for a job for him anyway? Can't he do it himself?"

"He doesn't know anybody in town. I just said I'd ask around a little." I didn't go on to say that if Truman didn't get himself gainfully employed, we'd be doing all our dating in Pop's projection booth.

"Well," he said thoughtfully, "you just go easy recommending someone like that. It'll reflect on you if Truman doesn't work out. I can understand your wanting to help him, and that's nice of you, but. . . ."

"Pop?"

"Yeah?"

"Do you think. . . ." I had to go slow and sort out my

words. "Do you think it's possible for a person to really be a good influence on somebody? I mean, like, somebody that seemed kind of good-for-nothing and headed nowhere. Would it be possible to be such a good influence on that person—you know, helping him get started in another direction—that you could really make a difference in his life?"

"I don't know, honey."

When I glanced up at him he had the saddest look on his face. I couldn't stand it. I left him and Adolf to each other's company and loped on home. The nice thing about having Mom home on weekends was having Mom's car home on weekends. She was on the phone with some friend from work and waved me toward the car keys without an argument.

I cruised through town trying to think of someplace Truman could get a job. Liberty is not much of a town. We're in the panhandle, midway between Fort Supply and Slapout, and not near enough to the oil fields for any noticeable wealth to have gilded our fair village. Highway 270 goes through the middle, and there's about two blocks of town on either side of the highway for maybe eight or ten blocks, and that's it: a couple of blocks of stores and bars, a water tower on one end and the grain elevator on the other, three churches and the Baptist Retirement Center.

I didn't realize I was looking for Don till I found his truck at the park. It's just a narrow little park where the Beaver River makes a loop close to the edge of town. There's a softball diamond and a shelter house and a rickety little dock where people put in fishing boats sometimes, or canoes.

Don and some other guys were lounging on each other's truck cabs, horsing around and swinging bats. From the amount of sweat being produced, I figured they'd been playing ball. I joined them.

"Who won?" I said.

"Game got called on account of the heat," Don said, bonking me easy on the top of my head. One bad thing about being so short, people are always doing things to the top of your head. I guess it's the only part of me they see.

Knowing the rules for times like this, I hung around but didn't interrupt while the guys finished off their horsing around and wandered away, all except Don.

"Can I talk to you?" I said to him when it looked as though he was heading for his truck too.

"I never knew you to not talk. But I got to get cool. Come on."

We walked down to the dock and I sat there while he pulled off his boots, handed me his pocket stuff—keys and money and knife—and waded into the river in his clothes. He got good and wet all over, then climbed up and sat beside me. Already the hot, dry air was sucking the river out of his jeans and shirt.

"What's on your little mind?"

"You know anybody around here that might give Truman Johnson a job, maybe on a ranch or whatever?"

"Nope."

"You're a big help."

"Well, you asked and I answered. From what I've heard

about that guy, I don't think I'd want to recommend him to any friends of mine. Especially not to any customers of mine."

Warming to the subject I said, "Yeah, but Don, if nobody ever gives him a chance, how is he ever going to get himself straightened out? So far he hasn't done anything all that bad, just selling a little marijuana at school and spending a few months in a correction place. It's not like he had a criminal record or anything."

He shot me a look heavy with doubt. "I heard you went out with him last night. You getting involved, Shortie?"

"No. I may be short, but I'm not stupid. All I'm trying to do here is to help him find a job. I had to do some talking to get him interested in looking for a job even, so I feel like. . . ." I didn't quite know what I meant.

"You feel like you're gonna be his guardian angel and make a new man out of him?"

It sounded stupid the way he said it, but I hung in there. "It's possible. Isn't it? I mean, to help someone at a crucial point in his life?"

He rolled over on his back and squinted from the sun. Man, he was good-looking.

"Shortie, take it from old Uncle Don. Trying to make somebody over is like roller skating over a dead cow. It can be done, but it ain't worth the effort."

On that heartening note I left and went looking for John Gray.

# 4

WHAT DO YOU THINK somebody named John Gray
would be like? Right. Perfect. Rich, handsome, and
genuinely kind, and how often do you find all that in
one man? He was slim for a man his age, with sort of
sandy coloring and incredibly tidy hair and clothes. He
always looked to me as if he'd just been polished.

He didn't seem to do anything specific for a living
except to be on boards of directors: the bank, the hospital,
who knows what all else. And his family owned or used to
own most of downtown Liberty, including the theater
building. The theater was closed for several years because
there wasn't enough business, but then John decided the
town needed it even if it lost money. That was about the
time when the railroad that used to go through Liberty
went broke and Pop, who had been a dispatcher, took
early retirement. Not that he had a choice. Anyway, somehow or other he and John knew each other, and John
hired him to run the theater. Pop liked taking care of the
place and running the machines, but he really didn't
want the responsibility of ordering films and the rest of
the business end of it, so John dug up Carol from somewhere and let her and Pop sort of split the job.

Now when a man's as busy and important as John Gray, you wouldn't expect him to care anything about small potatoes like Pop Kiffin, would you? But he honest-to-God does. And furthermore than that, he cares about me. At least he always made me feel like it was genuinely important to him how all the little details of my life were going. I know it's not just me—he's like that with every-body—but when I'm talking to him he makes me feel as if I must be important because John Gray is focusing on me.

So I didn't feel too terribly uncomfortable driving up his driveway on a Saturday afternoon, looking for him. His house is on the edge of town, way back behind a solid wood fence, like basket weave, with tall, skinny trees planted at even spaces all the way up the private road. The house kind of squats down in the shrubbery, and it doesn't look all that big till you drive around back and realize that it rambles forever around three sides of a pool.

Beyond the lawn area—lawn, not yard like my house—was a little stable and riding ring, where a beautiful girl was cantering around a jump course on a big gray hunter. I hadn't seen Marilee Gray since she went off to a private school in Virginia or some such place, but I knew she must be beautiful by now. What else could a man like John sire? I used to have fantasies that he was my father, but looking at Marilee and at myself, no. No way he could have produced the Afghan and the mutt both.

I found him sitting at a table under a beach umbrella, watching his daughter ride, or working among the papers on the table, or maybe both.

"Well, if it's not Miss California." He actually got up and shook my hand and sort of covered me with this warm glow of welcome. I could have sworn he'd been sitting there wishing for my company. "What brings you calling? Here, have a seat."

I'd hardly got lowered into the white wrought-iron chair on the other side of the table when the housekeeper was there with a bottle of Coke and a glass of shaved ice on a tray.

"I don't want to bother you if you're busy," I muttered, looking at the papers on the table.

"Nah, nothing important. How are things going for you? I hear you're working for Doc Fulcher this summer. Is that working out okay?"

See what I mean? Here's the most important man in town, and he's keeping track of me.

"It's not bad. I figure if I can stick it out all summer, I'll have about eight hundred to put down on a truck, and that'll be my biggest main expense. We might even go ahead and get the truck this year. Pop'd have to cosign for me, of course."

I rattled on awhile about my plans, till I realized I was doing it again. The bad thing about John is that he encourages me to talk about myself, which I love to do anyway, but then I'm always left with this selfish feeling, as though by being so nice to me he just proved he was a better person than I was. So I quit answering his questions and turned it around.

"I see Marilee is home for the summer. She graduated this year, didn't she?"

41

"Yes. She'll be going to Stevens in the fall. But don't worry, we're going to keep Shadrack." He twinkled his eyes at me. Shadrack was Marilee's horse, and when I first told John I was going to be a farrier he promised to be my first customer.

"John, I've got this friend—well, acquaintance—who needs a job, and I thought I'd just check with you, since you know everybody in the whole county."

He waited expectantly, so I went on. "It's Doc's new stepson, Truman Johnson."

"Oh. That one."

"He's really a nice guy, John. At least, from what I know of him. He's had some experience with ranch work, and he's willing to learn anything."

John looked dubious, and I wondered what he'd heard about Truman.

"Tell me, Callie, what do you think of him? Would you trust him?"

"Sure," I said because it was the expected thing, but I wasn't so sure, really. "Well, I think I would. I'm not saying he's overloaded with ambition or brains, but for ranch work or some such, I don't know why not. The thing is, he needs somebody to believe in him, John. I don't think he's ever had that before. He likes me, and he knows that I have confidence in him, that he can make something out of himself, and I don't think he'll let me down."

John twinkled at me again. "You going to be a sheero, are you?"

I got red, but we had a good laugh together anyhow. He teased me with that sheero thing a lot. Once, when I

42

was real little, after I'd been reading hero comics, I told Pop that when I grew up I was going to be a sheero. I figured if men were heros, women must be sheeros, right? What the heck, I was only five. Anyhow it got to be a joke between Pop and me, and he told it to John once. There are some things that they just won't let you forget.

"Yeah, John. I'm going to save him from himself." We were laughing, but part of me was serious.

"Well, then the least I can do is give you a hand. You send him out to the ranch Monday morning, and I'll tell Coop to put him to work. He can always use somebody out there."

I'd forgotten John owned a ranch. Naturally, he would, but it had slipped my mind. It was a smallish beef spread, small by Oklahoma standards anyhow, with a nice little set of buildings where Coop, the foreman, lived. I think it was some property that the bank got in a tax sale or some such.

I was so relieved about Truman I almost gave John a hug. Then remembered I was too old to do that anymore without raising eyebrows. I thanked him profusely, turned down his offer to stay and visit with Marilee, and drove home bursting to tell Truman that he was all fixed up.

Truman was less than thrilled. He showed up, on foot, around eight and we took off in Mom's car after promising to put some gas in it.

"You'll have to buy the gas," Truman said flatly as we pulled out of the driveway. "I've got exactly a buck and a half."

"But not for long," I bubbled. "You are now among

43

the army of the employed, as of Monday morning. I got you fixed up with a ranch-hand job! What do you think about them apples?"

Like I said, he wasn't thrilled, but he did agree to give it a try. I guess he was depressed at having run out of spending money. I hoped he was good and depressed. I even made a point of paying for the gas myself, at the station, instead of slipping him the money.

Since Pop wasn't working that night and we'd have had to pay admission, the movies were out. For a while we just drove around and talked, but I didn't want to do that all evening, not when I was buying the gas. Finally he parked in front of the Bum Steer Lounge.

"I don't think they'll let me in there," I said doubtfully. "I'm not eighteen."

"We can try. Just don't order beer or liquor. Or anything more than seventy-five cents."

"Right," I muttered, and helped myself out of the car. Chivalry was dead, or as near as makes no difference.

I'd never been in a bar before. It was dark, with a lot of gleaming wood and big Hamms' Beer signs that were lighted forest scenes with rivers that really rippled. I liked the signs. The people were mostly guys, in jeans and boots and plaid shirts, and a few women who looked pretty ordinary. Kind of cheap-ordinary, if you know what I mean, but that might have been the lighting.

It was a good thing I wasn't intimidated by my first venture into the underworld, since my date evaporated as soon as we were through the door. I looked around a little, sort of waiting to see if I was going to get thrown out, but nothing happened. Toward the back of the room

44

were two doors marked BULLS and HEIFERS. Their clever way of labeling the rest rooms, I figured. I hid out in Heifers for a few minutes while I kind of got myself oriented, but somebody was rattling the doorknob and probably needed the room worse than I did, so I went back out again.

There was the bar along one side, and a few tables across the front, and three or four video games and a big pool table. Truman appeared with a Coke for me and a beer for himself, then faded off again to watch the pool game. I stood around feeling dumb and thinking that dating wasn't living up to its advertising.

After a while I realized Truman was playing pool with a guy named Harlan something. I'd seen him working in the Chevron station, with HARLAN on his uniform shirt. He had the greasiest black hair I've ever seen, bar none. Looked as though he used his head for a dipstick. It was a little, narrow head, way too little for the rest of him. He looked like a creep and probably was.

Another thing dawned on me as the marvelously exciting evening wore on: Truman was betting. Money. He played several games with Harlan and then a few more with Harlan's buddy, Eddy something-or-other, who was fat and pale and had horrible skin. I didn't stand too close to the pool table because I didn't want to get in their way, and I also didn't much want the whole town knowing who I was with. But from what they were yelling and whooping, it sounded like ten-dollar bets floating around.

"Maybe he's an incredibly talented pool shark," I told myself, "and he's going to clean out the local yokels."

It didn't quite work out that way, but by the time he

tore himself away to take me home he was fifteen dollars ahead of the nothing he started with. And crowing! I was less than crowing. I was dead on my feet. There was nowhere to sit in that place, and I'd been standing for over three hours by the time my let's-go hints got through to him.

"Fifteen bucks, tax free, just for playing a game," he gloated. "See, Cal? You don't have to slave away at some stupid job to make money. There are better ways."

"Uh-uh," I growled. "You were betting money you didn't have, stud. If you'd lost instead of won, that would have been a different story."

"Oh, you'd have come to my rescue, wouldn't you?"

We'd pulled into the driveway by then, and he put his arms around me and aimed a kiss in my direction, but I wasn't having any.

"You thought I'd have loaned you money? Think again, Truman. I went out of my way to get you a job, and I'll help you in any way I can in that direction, but I'm not paying your debts, so you can just forget that."

He softened and got serious then and started looking like a rejected puppy. "I thought you were my friend," he said in a kind of crackly little voice.

"Aww. . . ."

He kissed me a good one then, and something flopped over inside me. It was as though I was dedicating myself to him.

He drew me in against him and kind of whispered, "Cal, you're the only friend I've got, you know that? Mom and I never got along, and Doc hates my guts."

"No, he doesn't."

"Well, he's got no use for me, let's put it that way. And I never did have any close friends at Tumbleweed. Everybody was out for themselves all the time at that place, trying to survive themselves, and to hell with the other guy. I was about convinced I was thoroughly worthless, you know? And then there's little Callie, actually caring whether I live or die."

"Aww—"

"I mean it. You going out and finding me that job, you don't know what that means to me."

"I didn't think you were all that hot to get a job."

"Well, what I meant was, how much it meant that you would do something like that for me, that you'd care enough to, see?"

For the first time I could ever remember I had the sensation of someone needing me. He was looking deep into my eyes, as if he was testing to see if he could really depend on me, and I knew right then that I would never let him down.

I was still about half-dazed by it all when he left and I went into the house. Part of my mind noticed that he was walking the wrong way, heading back toward town rather than toward Doc's house, but it didn't register.

The house was mostly dark. Pop's room was the little square room behind the living room, where he'd been sleeping since Mom started working nights. It was kind of a den in the daytime but it had a foldout sofa bed, and he slept in there so he and Mom wouldn't wake each other up coming and going. It was dark back there, and the lump of him was in bed. I could see the shape against the moonlight in the window behind him. I'd figured he'd

47

stay awake till I was safely home, and it ticked me off just a little to see that he hadn't.

The two upstairs rooms were Mom's and mine, with just a narrow little bit of hallway in between. She was awake. The light was on and her TV set was going. She never could get to sleep on her nights off till way late. Going past her door I held my breath. I really didn't want to have to tell her about my lovely evening at the Bum Steer Lounge and Pool Hall. But she wasn't much for midnight mother-daughter chats anyhow, so I was safe enough.

I closed my own door and, leaving the lights off, kicked out of my clothes, turned on the window fan, and flopped out on the bed to think about Truman.

Being needed by another person. Wow. Fantastic. It was so different from just being loved, like by parents. I mean, that's nice, but then they have to love you if they're your parents. But here was a whole other person who hadn't even known me this time last week, and now here I was, the most important person in his life. I loved it!

I rolled over and got an armful of pillow and started planning ahead. Now, just between you and me, I talk a good game, but deep down in my private mind I'm not all that sure about me—I mean, how I measure up to other people. I can tell about where I stand in my class at school, somewhere around the middle. Not brilliant, not dumb. But the things that are important to me, like learning my trade, I'm smart at that. When Don explains stuff to me, like how you angle a back hoof to correct a breakover fault, I can see that right away. And it didn't take me any time at all to learn how to use his acetylene forge. And

48

when people crack jokes I always get them, even when Shelly is still standing there with her mouth open, trying to figure it all out.

So I think I'm okay in the smarts department. And I *think* most people like me. I'm terrible honest, and I know that makes some people uncomfortable, but the people who matter like me for it. And people trust me. That's important. Carol never checks the ticket numbers when she leaves me selling tickets at the theater; she knows I'm not about to cheat her.

But when it comes to love and romance and all that, I get scared a lot, thinking about it. I know, I kid around a lot about how I'd have grabbed Don if Juanita hadn't got to him first, but just between us and the fence post, I know he'd never fall in love with me. I'm just not the type that guys feel that way about. I'm not helpless enough, and I'm sure not going to fake it.

And John Gray doesn't count. I flatter myself that he cares about me, but I know darn well he treats everybody the same way. He's the same with Carol, and Pop, and the whole town, so I can't take any credit for him being a friend of mine.

I used to get crushes on different guys at school, including the men teachers, but I never told anybody about them. If I told Shelly, she'd probably have gone out and got the guy for herself just to prove she could. And who wants the whole world to know that there's not a single boy in the whole school that's interested in you? Not this kid. People would feel sorry for me, which is the same as feeling superior, and I can't take that.

So I just never said anything to anybody. But now,

here was Truman. No great prize, sure, but maybe there were possibilities there, you know? Maybe the thing for somebody like me to do was to get a guy like Truman, that nobody else much wanted, and then make him into somebody good. I already got him a job, didn't I? If I could gradually work him around to shaving off that stupid beard and carrying himself more proud like, he might be an okay guy.

And a few years down the pike, heck, he might be doing so well out there on John's ranch that when Coop retired, Truman would take over as manager. That was a nice little house out there, and I could run my business from there. . . .

Possibilities.

# 5

I WOKE UP in a kind of glow. It was as if I had a wonderful, praiseworthy new mission in life. Years from now, when Truman Johnson was a prominent and respected citizen of Liberty, a successful rancher or whatever, he was going to look back on his life and tell people, "If it hadn't been for California Kiffin, I'd have gone bad for sure."

In my vision he was living in a sprawling ranch house with basket-weave fencing and a pool, and his daughter was riding her hunter through a jump course in the back forty.

But then the vision blurred up considerably. What would a man like that be doing with a wife that shod horses for a living?

I rolled over on my back and laughed out loud. Here I was, going from Truman being a pool-hall bum barely good enough to be seen in public with to making him into a John Gray that I wasn't good enough for. You can't accuse me of not having imagination.

Pop was outside, under my window, talking to somebody—his new puppy I saw when I finally got myself upright and looked out. He had Adolf on a leash and was walking him around the outside edge of our yard, showing him his territory. Pop had a dream of some day owning a dog that wouldn't go out of the yard. It was on a par with my dream of making something out of that sow's ear of a Truman, I reckoned, grinning at myself in the mirror as I beat my hair into submission.

Mom was sleeping in, as usual. Pop and Adolf met me in the kitchen, where Pop had his pancake makings laid out. It was our Sunday morning tradition. He made them real little and real thin, called them dollar flapjacks because they weren't much bigger than a silver dollar. But good? Man! They had little crunchies all around the edges and none of that doughy stuff you get in the middle of big pancakes.

He got to work on them and I sat at the table, my stomach growling already. "How'd Adolf make it through his first night?" I patted my knee and the pup came wriggling up my leg for an ear rubbing.

"Not bad," Pop said cheerfully. "One puddle, but other than that he was a good ole pupper."

"Sleep in bed with you?" I teased.

"Well, his first night in a strange house, what do you expect? He don't take up much room, little mutt like that. Do you, Adolf? You hang on a minute. We'll have some pancake scraps for you."

I braced my feet on the other chair and studied Pop from the back while he dropped a drop of water in the skillet to test the sizzle. There was something about that stocky little shape and the boyishness in the back of his

52

neck that made me sad all of a sudden. I thought about Mom sleeping upstairs with her television set and him sleeping on that hide-a-bed in the den with nobody to hug but a dog, and for a second there it made me want to bawl.

I thought back to before Mom was working and our family was more normal, Pop going off to work every day and her sitting around watching game shows or going to garage sales with her friends. Did she love Pop? Ever? Was there ever a time that I could remember when she gave him a loving look or put her arms around him?

I didn't think so. Teasing, yes. She was always teasing him about something, usually about how short he was, making jokes, and he'd laugh, but when I thought about it now, it seemed like there was a cutting edge in her jokes and Pop was bleeding inside from them.

Pop's real name is Jimmy, and sometimes in my head I call him Jiminy Cricket, or I used to when I was littler. I must have heard it from Mom. When I thought it, it seemed like a loving nickname, but coming from her, I wasn't so sure.

He looked like a Jiminy Cricket this morning though, bouncing over to the table to lay before me my plate of dollar flapjacks. He always filled my plate first, then made a second batch for himself. Usually I pigged into mine while he was still cooking, but today I held off till he sat down with me. Maybe that was to make up for his having to sleep with a dachshund.

"How was your date last night?" he asked, drizzling honey over his stack.

"Marvelous. We went to the Bum Steer and I got to stand around for three hours watching him play pool. He won fifteen dollars, betting with money he didn't have, and came away convinced that only fools work for a living. I think it's going to be uphill work reforming this one."

He stopped eating and gave me a long, uncomfortable look. "You were in the Bum Steer?"

"Yeah, why?"

"Well," he kind of sputtered, "that's not the kind of place you should be going into, Callie. You're underage, for one thing."

"I know. I didn't drink anything but Coke."

"But that's a rough place, darlin'. I don't want my little girl hanging around in places like that. This is a small town, don't forget. It won't do your reputation any good."

His attitude tilted me up on my hind legs. I guess I shouldn't have been surprised. It was a perfectly fatherly way for him to feel, when I thought about it. And I know Mom probably would have disapproved. But somehow he had never disapproved of anything I'd ever done, that I could remember. He'd always been on my side, through bad report cards, through the time I skipped school to go out to the fairgrounds to watch them set up for the rodeo. It shook me up to have him disapproving of me now.

"Look," I said, a little shrill, "I didn't want to go there, I didn't know we were going there, and I sure as heck didn't enjoy myself. But I don't see what you're getting all bent out of shape about, Pop. It's a local bar. I didn't hear any words in there that I haven't known since sixth grade, and there were hardly any white slavers hanging

54

around. Mostly people like Lou and Ethel Gorsuch, sitting around the bar having a few beers on a Saturday night."

"I know. But Lou and Ethel Gorsuch aren't a seventeen-year-old girl with a spotless reputation who hopes to make a living in this town and who needs to be well thought of."

He had me there.

"And this Truman kid," Pop said more slowly, "I'm just not too sure he's the kind you'd ought to be hanging around with, darlin'. He sounds like a loser to me."

"But he's not going to be a loser long," I chirped. "I got him a job! I went out and talked to John Gray yesterday afternoon, Pop, and he told me to send Truman out to the ranch Monday morning. He'd tell Coop to put him to work. Isn't that great? See? Just a little help from his friends is all Truman was needing."

Pop put down his fork and his face got so red I got up and reached toward him, thinking he was choking.

"You went out and asked John Gray for a favor like that, after I told you how I felt about it?"

"Pop, you were the one that suggested John, if you remember. What are you getting mad at me for? It was your idea."

He simmered down some. "I reckon I did bring up his name when you first asked, but if you recall, I went on to say I didn't want you bothering John asking for jobs for your friends unless you were sure they'd be good employees, and hon, from what you've been saying about this Truman, especially him taking you to that place last night and all that betting and pool business, I just don't like it at all."

"Don't like what? Me trying to do Truman a favor?"

"Your taking advantage of John's good nature like that. He's gone out of his way for this family more than once, and I don't like being in his debt any more than necessary."

"But he didn't mind. He was nice about it."

"Of course he was nice about it. He's always nice about everything, and that's why people tend to take advantage of him, and I don't want my family doing it."

"So okay, I won't anymore," I muttered. We finished our breakfast in stony silence.

But it was hard on us. I kept sneaking little peeks at him while we read the Sunday paper over the mess of our pushed-back breakfast dishes. He looked the way I felt. I couldn't remember the last time we'd been mad at each other. If I could have thought of any way to lighten things up, I would have.

He did it finally. He looked up from the classified ads section with the old Jiminy Cricket grin and said, "I know what let's do today. Let's you and me go over to Fort Supply and look at pickup trucks."

"You mean to buy?" My eyes got big.

"No, just window-shopping. For fun. You want to? If you're thinking about getting your truck later on this year, you'd ought to know what the going prices are, hadn't you? Unless you got something else you were going to do today?"

I could see in his eyes how much he didn't want me to have anything I'd rather do. And besides, I honestly couldn't think of any way I'd rather spend the day.

We took off in high spirits, both of us relieved that the mad was over. Adolf stood on my lap with his nose out

56

the window, eyes closed and ears flying. I had to keep hold of him so he didn't climb clear out and blow away.

The first car lot we went to was closed Sundays, but we walked around anyhow and looked in the windows of the four used pickups at the back of the lot. It was fun looking at them and imagining this one or that one being my future place of business, but there weren't any of them that would have been just right for me, which was fine, since we were only looking anyhow. The new ones were gorgeous, all except for those five-digit price tags. We boosted Adolf back into the car and drove on.

The next place was open. I decided I liked shopping at closed lots better. This one was crawling with salesmen who just flat out didn't believe Pop when he said we were only looking, not buying today, thank you very much. They came at us in relays, asking what we had for a trade-in and what price range were we thinking about and wouldn't we like to just take a look at the new three-quarter-ton Ranger Deluxe in the showroom. I'd have sicced Adolf on them if I'd thought anybody would take Adolf seriously. I did give a silent cheer when that good little ole puppy lifted his leg on a wire-spoked hubcap. It must have been the first time in his young life that he'd lifted instead of squatted because he almost tipped over backward in the attempt, so I figured it was his commentary on car salesmen.

Eventually they left us alone and turned their attention to a more promising shopper, and we headed for the cheaper old cars and trucks at the far end of the lot.

Do you believe in love at first sight? Well, I do now. I saw it and I knew it was mine. It was a metallic blue half-ton Chevy with a blue-and-white fiberglass shell, just like what I'd need to protect my tools, my acetylene forge and supplies of shoes and nails, and my split-leg cowhide apron—all the things I had picked out in the farrier-supply catalog. The stuff dreams are made of.

I walked around the truck while Pop watched me fall in love. It had mud flaps with appaloosa horses on them. According to the decals on the windows of the shell, the former owner belonged to the Oklahoma Aps Club, the Sunset Trail Riders, and the Southwest Charolais Breeders Association. All of which seemed to mean that this was my truck, planned by fate.

The price tag on the windshield said thirty-seven fifty. I didn't like looking at it. Pop and I climbed inside, and I stroked the steering wheel.

"Only got eighteen thousand miles on her," Pop said, just as if we were really considering. . . .

"Sure wish I was rich instead of merely beautiful," I said, sighing.

For a while more we played around with the truck, looking in the glove compartment and under the seats and commenting on this and that, but then a salesman found us and started in on why didn't we take it out for a test drive and wouldn't it be just the ticket for whatever we wanted it for.

"You don't even know what we do want a truck for," I finally said. I couldn't help it.

Pop said, "My daughter here is going to be a farrier when she gets out of school. She'll be needing a truck to work out of, when the time comes."

He sounded so proud.

The salesman got a blank look on his face. Pop and I knew darn well he didn't even know what a farrier was. We got away from him and back into our own car and broke up laughing.

"Do you want to go look at any more?" he asked after we got our breath back.

"Nah, I don't think so. That blue one. . . ."

I looked back at it over my shoulder as we drove away. Pop patted my knee and said, "Maybe it'll still be there by the end of the summer when you've got enough to swing the down payment. Or if not, there'll be another one just as good. You hungry?"

"When was I ever not hungry?"

"Right."

We stopped at Arbie's and got roast beef sandwiches sliced thin and piled high and took them to the little roadside park at the edge of Fort Supply. We tied Adolf's leash to the door handle and sat on top of the picnic table with our feet on the bench and the food between us and feasted. It was a nice little park, just a turnaround and a rest room building, but it was sheltered from the highway by a stand of oaks, and nobody else was there, so it was like our own little private park.

I'd never felt closer to Pop than I did right then, for some reason.

"Pop?"

"Hm."

"I just decided I'm not ever going to get married. I'd never find anybody as nice to me as you are. I'll just be a withered up old maid, devoting my life to caring for my elderly father."

"What do you reckon your elderly mother's going to be doing all this time?" He said it with a smile in his voice.

"Taking care of herself, I expect."

I knew right away I'd hurt him, but I didn't know just how. "Only kidding."

He smiled and motioned me toward the cardboard boat of French fries, with ketchup all over his half but not mine. See what I mean about him being good to me?

"Pop. . . ."

He said nothing, so I went on. "How come you married Mom?"

He laughed, embarrassed. "Same reason everybody gets married, I reckon."

"Because their girl friend is pregnant?"

He went kind of stiff. It occurred to me that we'd never talked about this, and he didn't know how much I knew. I didn't want to hurt him talking about it, but I wanted to know him better. I guess I was hoping there was some wonderful deep love between him and Mom that I couldn't see. All day, in the back of my mind, I'd been carrying around that picture of him falling asleep with his arm around his puppy, just like some little boy that nobody loves.

"What makes you say that, Callie?"

I wadded up my sandwich wrappings and hook-shot them into the trash barrel. "I've known about it for years. But it's okay. I know somebody else is my genetic father, but you're my real one. You know that." I wanted to soothe it for him as much as I could.

He just sat there.

"The only reason I was asking," I said finally, "is that I wondered about you and Mom—you know, whether you guys really love each other, or if you ever did, or what the deal is. She just never seems like she *gives* you anything, you know?"

"She gave me you," he said quietly.

I moved the French fries and skootched over where he could hug me up to him, and we sat there looking off into the tree branches. It seemed as if the only way we could talk to each other was by bouncing it off the tree branches.

"Did you love her, Pop?"

"Always. And I've never stopped. Honey, when I first met Norma she was the prettiest and the sweetest girl I'd ever seen. And I still see her that way."

"She must have been a lot younger than you. I mean—"

He laughed a little. "Twenty years between us. But it wasn't that so much. It was everything else. There she was, looking like Elizabeth Taylor, and there I was, as homely as a box of rocks. And shorter than her. And not ever going to get rich working for the railroad. I never felt like I had any right to even ask her out."

"Where did you meet her?"

"Just kept seeing her around. You know how it is in a town this size. You don't ever meet people, you just start seeing them more often—mostly at the bowling alley, in this case. She and her girl friends used to go down there on Friday nights, and then so did I, as soon as I figured out that's where she'd be. More often than not they'd leave with somebody, men, and I'd go home kicking myself for not having the nerve to ask her to go with me. But I never did."

61

"So what happened?"

He shrugged and clamped me a little tighter against his ribs. "We got to be friends, gradual. I guess she figured I was so little and homely that I wasn't even in the running for her serious attention, so that made me a safe friend. And I think she knew I'd never hurt her in any way, nor let anybody else hurt her if I could help it."

"Didn't you ever take her out?"

"Oh, sometimes if her girl friends would get lucky and she didn't—they'd take off with guys and kind of leave Norma stranded—then she'd take up with me and bowl a game or let me take her for something to eat and then I'd drive her home. But I never got fresh or anything like that."

I smiled down toward my lap. That sounded so much like him. I poked him with my elbow to get the story going again.

"Well, then, one night she was there but she wasn't bowling, said she didn't feel good, and she looked awful. So I offered to take her for a drive and before I knew it she was crying all over me and telling me she wanted to marry me."

"She tell you she was pregnant?"

He shook his head. I could feel his chin against my scalp. "She never once told me. We got married that next weekend, and seven months later I had my baby daughter, and she never said a thing."

The pain was rich in his voice.

"Did she think you were stupid, or what? She should have at least been honest with you."

He said nothing.

"What I never have been able to figure out, though," I said cautiously, not wanting to hurt him any more than I had to, "is how come she treats you the way she does? I mean, she acts like you did something awful to her, instead of the other way around. How come?"

His hand gripped and patted my bicep. There was a smile in his voice, a warmth that I loved. "That's human nature, darlin'. You always hate the people you're indebted to. They make you feel small, no matter how hard they try not to. All I ever wanted to do was make her life better, and I did that for her, but she knows deep down that I treated her more fair than she treated me, so she feels like she's a bad person compared to me, and she resents that. Besides, you can't be grateful to anybody very long without it getting to be an awful burden."

I thought about that. It made sense.

"But would she have been better off if you hadn't married her?" I asked slowly.

He sighed. "I expect she'd have turned out unhappy no matter what she'd have done. She's just one of those people who can't be comfortable in life unless they're unhappy about something or other."

"The great philosophies of James W. Kiffin."

We chuckled and stretched and fed Adolf our scraps and headed home.

# 6

I DIDN'T SEE TRUMAN all week, but then I didn't expect to. He was leaving early every morning for the ranch and getting back, apparently, after I left the office and jogged home. I didn't mind not seeing him. In fact, it was easier to concentrate on learning my job without Truman always drooping around the place. And I loved the thought of him out there on John's ranch, sweating the sweat of honest toil and piling up that hourly wage.

On Tuesday I got to help deliver three Boston terrier puppies by caesarian surgery, and I got so interested in it that I didn't get woozy at all. On Wednesday Doc let me give shots to a dog and trim its toenails. Of course the owner was waiting out front and didn't realize it wasn't Doc doing the work. If I'd been the owner I'd have raised hell about it, but it was fun getting to do that stuff.

Thursday night I went over to Fort Supply to the hospital with Don to see his new baby girl that had been born the day before. Was he ever thrilled! You'd think he'd done the hard part. It was sweet to see him and Juanita with their heads bent over that little scrap of a baby and looking at each other as though they knew the secret of the universe and nobody else was in on it. But I have to admit it gave me a cold feeling for a minute there, like an orphan in a snowstorm, looking in somebody's window. So I went down to the hospital basement, to the huge old kitchen down there, and talked to Mom awhile till Don was ready to head for home.

Actually, talking to Mom in those circumstances didn't make me feel much less orphanny. Get her in her uniform, in those surroundings, and she's a different person from the sleepy frump I usually see slouching around the kitchen at home. Down there she's all tidy and straight and brisk, and she has people working under her. Two other women on the night shift have to do what she tells them. She's the head honcho, and when I see her down there I get impressed, in spite of myself.

I mean, I love Pop so much, and I hate the way she is toward him, but on the other hand when I see her in action she seems so much, well, stronger than Pop. Smarter, I suppose, although I hate to put it that way. It doesn't seem logical that she should be married to him. And if I can see that, even from where I sit, just think how much clearer it must be to her. And to him.

Then how come she's stayed married to him all these years? Out of gratitude for him marrying her? What an awful reason to stay married to somebody for seventeen years.

But I couldn't talk about it with her. We didn't know each other that well. We talked about Don and Juanita's baby, and I told her about my caesarian section, and she

65

asked if Adolf was still making puddles in the night, and then I just sort of sat around on the stool in the corner of the kitchen while Mom worked on cinnamon rolls.

Do you know how much dough it takes for three hundred cinnamon rolls? An armful, let me tell you.

It was a good week, one of the best I've ever had. My head was full of warm thoughts about Truman, with layers of other warm thoughts about a summer's worth of paychecks and that blue pickup truck with signs on the doors that said, C. J. KIFFIN, FARRIER, LIBERTY, OKLAHOMA. But mostly I thought about Truman.

It's funny how much better looking he got that week by staying out of sight. You know how the guy changes into the werewolf in the movies, with hair sprouting and fangs stretching, right before your eyes? My mental picture of Truman did something like that in reverse that week. The beard and the slouch melted away and he darkened into a slim, hard cowboy type with kind eyes filled with gentle love.

Not knowing whether he'd be working Saturdays or not, I wasn't sure whether to expect a date Friday night or not until Saturday, but I figured we'd be getting together sometime on the weekend, so I bounced all the way to work Friday, full of that old Friday joy.

During the school year I'd get almost crazy with light-headedness on Fridays. It wasn't so much that I hated school, I just hated the confinement of it. The work wasn't all that hard, just boring, and there were times when I felt like I'd scream if I had to sit another ten minutes in those hard, confining little wooden desks. Especially when

66

the weather was nice outside. You take one of those bronzy days in October or November, or one of those greeny-gold days in April. Well, it's against human nature to have to be inside on days like that.

I perfected the art of looking out school windows by just slanting my eyes toward them, not turning my whole head. That way nobody knew my mind wasn't where it was supposed to be. But there'd be such a restlessness in me, building up through the week, that by Fridays I'd feel like I'd been tied up and grain-fed and my skin couldn't hold me in.

It was like that now, not because I wanted to escape from the job at Doc's so much as I wanted the excitement of seeing Truman tonight or tomorrow night and hearing him say he was getting the hang of his job and liking it, and that it sure felt good to be earning honest money. Then, I figured, my job of getting him on the right track would be pretty much over with, and we could relax and enjoy one another.

Friday afternoon about two, Doc called me into the treatment room where he was getting ready to crop ears on a litter of Doberman puppies. I figured he needed a hand with something, but he said he was going to be tied up with Doberman ears for quite a while and would I take the week's receipts to the bank since he didn't want to leave that much money around over the weekend.

I walked the three blocks to the bank thinking how great it was going to be to have my pickup to drive around town on little errands like this. Having your own pickup is the separation point between the women and the girls, believe me. I could feel it in my mind, how it was going to be to have those keys in my hand, those wheels at my beck and call—whatever a beck is.

Driver's training was the one class that held my attention last year, because it was teaching me something I needed to know to run my business. No matter how much they try to tell you that we learn valuable lessons from the past, you'll never convince me that memorizing the dates of the Crimean and Boer wars is going to make me a better farrier. But driver's training, that was something else.

The bank is about the classiest building in Liberty. It's got diagonal redwood paneling and red velvety wallpaper and all that stuff.

I made the deposit, folded up the empty plastic zipper pouch and wadded it into my pocket, and was standing there in the lobby debating whether to go back to the loan department and sound them out about financing pickup trucks for seventeen-year-old girls, when I saw John Gray coming out of the big room where they have their board-of-directors' meetings, back behind the teller cages. He was talking with some other guy, so all I was going to do was wave and say, "Hi," but when he saw me he excused himself from the other guy and came over to me.

"Callie," he said.

"Hi, John."

"Listen," he said in an earnest voice, "I just wanted to tell you I felt badly about how things worked out with your friend, and that there's no—"

"What do you mean? What friend?"

"That boy. Truman."

"What are you talking about? Isn't he doing a good job?" I felt it coming in the pit of my stomach.

John looked surprised. "You mean you didn't know? He only stayed on the job a day and a half."

"He quit?!" I stared at John, drop-jawed.

He nodded in that kind way of his. "Apparently he didn't take kindly to Coop giving him orders."

"But he never said anything. He's been taking off every morning and coming home every night, and he's been telling Doc about all the stuff he was doing out there. Heck, John, he's been feeding us a load of—"

John kind of smiled and steered me out the door with his arm around my shoulder. I had the feeling he didn't want me letting loose my language in that classy bank. "Callie, let me give you a few little words of wisdom, learned in my old age, okay? All of the men in this world aren't princes, like me and your pop."

"I know that."

"All right. Just so you pick and choose. The Trumans of this world aren't worth bothering about generally, and you'll only get yourself hurt or in trouble if you mess around with them. Take it from your kindly old Uncle John."

I stopped and turned and squinted up at him. "But I've got to have faith in Truman. He needs me. Nobody's ever needed me before, John. If I go back on him, then he's going to go to the dogs for sure. I'm not blaming you. You did everything you could. I'll just have to try to find him a job he'll like better, that's all."

69

His face lost its joking look. "Leave him alone, hon. Don't waste yourself on somebody like that."

One thing I decided for sure while I clomped that three blocks back to the office: I wasn't going to take anybody's word except Truman's for why he quit that job. My first mad was burning off by then, and I began to feel sorry for Truman, having to pretend to go off to work every day just so he wouldn't have to let Yvonne and Doc down. And me. I could guess how bad he felt about only lasting a day and a half on his first real job. I'd have to get to him as soon as I could and let him know I was still on his side.

Before I left the office that night I gave Doc a message for Truman. "Tell him to come over to my house tonight. I need to talk to him. It's important." Then I jogged home, waving at the Egglestons but not looking at them. When Pop asked me if I had plans for the evening or if I wanted to come down to his projection booth and watch the movie with him, I said I thought I had a date with Truman. He gave me a look, as though he wanted to ask questions but was afraid to. I left the room.

Seven o'clock. Truman probably hadn't had time to get supper eaten and get cleaned up. No sweat.

Eight. Any time now. I went out and sat on the front steps for a while but the bugs were too bad and I had to go back in.

By nine, I was mad. I tromped through the backyard and across the empty house's yard and across the street and past Egglestons' and through Doc's yard and up to his back door and knocked. Loud.

Yvonne answered the door. When I said I wanted to talk to Truman, she sort of sputtered and spattered at me and said he'd gone out right after supper. With me, she thought.

"Wrong." I stepped inside and said to Doc, who was coming through the kitchen to see what was up, "Did Truman say anything to you about what he's been doing all this week?" I kept my voice level, but it wasn't easy.

"Doing?" Doc said. "What do you mean, doing? He's been working. Hasn't he?"

"You better ask him," I muttered, not quite wanting to be the one to tell on him, but not wanting him to be getting away with this junk either. "Sorry I bothered you."

I was going to go home, but on a sudden notion I turned toward downtown and commenced to jog. Might as well be building up my strength for when I lit into that rat, I figured.

Going into the Bum Steer with Truman was one thing. Going in alone was something else again, I realized as I got close. I wiped my palms on my jeans legs, sucked in my gut, and straight-armed into the place.

Nobody much noticed. I snaked through the crowd of beer drinkers and joke-tellers and lie-swappers, looking for my shaggy skeleton with the anemic beard. He wasn't there. Neither were the two guys he'd been playing pool with last weekend, Eddie and Harlan or whatever the heck their names were.

As soon as I was sure Truman wasn't there, I got out and, since I couldn't think of anyplace else to go hunting Truman, I slopped on down to the theater and watched

71

the movie awhile. Good old Pop. He never said word one about what happened to my date. He just went downstairs and brought us up a cardboard tray of popcorn with extra butter and Cokes, and we watched the movie without talking.

Saturday morning, small animal time. As Doc explained to me, he tried to lump all the small animal appointments together on that one day, to get the danged nuisances out of the way. The real profits were in the ranch calls. He could make more in one day castrating calves than in a whole week of distemper shots, although I had to wonder about that, seeing what the markup on the distemper shots was. Once I asked him if he ripped off the small animal customers every chance he got just to make up for the lack of profit from the dogs and cats in general, as compared to ranch stock. He just gave me a half-cocked grin and left me to draw my own conclusions, which I did.

Up until now I'd always been a firm believer in the fact that crime doesn't pay, but the more I got to know about Doc's finances, the more I had to wonder.

About midmorning Sedge Critz came in for a carton of prescription dog food for his over-the-hill Schnauzer who has kidney problems. Sedge owns the drugstore, where he dispenses gossip more than anything else.

He's a kind of dust-colored old bird, bent over probably from listening in on conversations through the paperback book racks. He could be anywhere from forty to two hundred years old.

I got him the carton of K/D and said, as I was writing up the charge, "What's new in town?"

"Trouble over to the car wash," he said, as if he was offering pearls beyond price. "D'you hear about it?"

"No. What? Change machines get ripped off again?" I parked on the corner of my desk and gave him my attention. Gossip is fun, let's face it.

"Yeah, but with class this time." He leered. "Some dude went and made photocopies of dollar bills and run them through the change machine. Bob went to empty the machine this morning and found all the quarters was gone and nothing but these fake photocopies of dollar bills inside. Mad? I tell you, he was fit to be tied. Had the sheriff and two deputies out there, eight o'clock this morning. Not that there's anything they can do about it, not unless they happen upon some dude with thirty-seven dollars' worth of quarters in his jeans."

I don't think I need to tell you what was going through my mind at that moment, do I? Sedge went out chuckling as if he hadn't heard anything so funny since the hogs ate Aunt Nancy.

When we closed up shop at noon I asked Doc if Truman was over at the house. He said no, he reckoned Truman was working today.

Uh-uh.

I was about at the point where I wanted to tell Pop what Truman was doing, or might be doing, but this was Pop's Saturday to work the kiddie matinee, and he just barely had time between sweeping out the Friday night trash from under the theater seats and threading up the first of the Roadrunner cartoons to grab a quick bite of lunch.

For a while I kicked around the house, but I was too

antsy to stay in there, dodging Mom's notice and tripping over Adolf, so I went downtown and just walked up and down, looking in windows, watching for Yvonne's car with Truman in it. Finally, figuring anything was better than doing nothing, I went into the Bum Steer.

It was startlingly dark in there after the glare of the sidewalk outside. Only a couple of guys sat at the far end of the bar talking to the bartender. I forced myself into casual gear and went up to them.

"Any of you guys know where I can find Truman Johnson?"

Blank looks.

"Okay then, how about Harlan or Eddie? You know, they play pool in here?"

It was a long shot. One evening of pool doth not a friendship make, but on the other hand Truman was out somewhere today, and it darn sure wasn't John Gray's ranch, and who else did he know around here?

"You mean Harlan Wilke?" the bartender said.

I shrugged. "I guess so. Black hair, works in the Chevron station?" It occurred to me then that I should have tried the station. I said I was adorable, I didn't promise you smart.

"Harlan Wilke, that's him. He lives out past Lizard Bridge, I think. Junky old place. That Eddie, I know who you mean, but I don't know nothing about him."

Lizard Bridge. Wonderful. My day really needed Lizard Bridge. I sighed and thanked the boys and headed for home and Mom's car. First I took it to the Chevron station for a small drink of gas and to see if Harlan was working today. He wasn't. And when I asked the guy that owned the place, he said Harlan hadn't been in all week and therefore probably didn't work there anymore.

I didn't like the sound of that.

"Do you know where he lives?"

"Out past Lizard Bridge. First place, I believe."

Wonderful.

Lizard Bridge is a rattletrap old railroad bridge about three miles south of town, on a dirt road. It crosses Lizard Creek, and when I was little it was the testing ground for the manhood and womanhood of the third grade set. If you could walk across it stepping on every other tie, you were okay. Crawling on hands and knees didn't count. I always figured any little kid who could pump a bike for three miles in that heat on that old dirt road had already proved herself.

But besides the bridge there was a little ghost town out there, just three old false-fronted store buildings and a post office. There weren't even any houses anymore. They got vandalized to death, I expect.

I drove through the town and across the road bridge, which wasn't a whole lot sturdier than the railroad bridge, then slowed down to start looking for Harlan's place.

And there it was, in all its glory. Mostly what you could see from the road was a jumble of stock pens made out of rusty wire and rotting planks and whatever was handy, including old car tires and concrete blocks. There were a couple of sheds and a more-or-less house sitting way back behind the junk.

Parked between the sheds and the house was a derelict

old Cadillac Coup de Ville that had been baby blue before cancer set in. It had air shocks on it, who knows why, and they were inflated so its rear end stuck up in the air.

And right there beside it, cozy as could be, was Yvonne Fulcher's green Plymouth.

Mad? I just barely caught myself in time to keep from slamming the car door when I got out. I marched up to that place fit to wring Truman's neck, or at least dead set on telling that creep what I thought of him.

At the door, I started to raise my hand to knock, but I could see somebody in there, so I cupped my hands around my eyes for shade and looked in.

There sat the man of my dreams, big as life, at the kitchen table with Harlan Wilke on the other side of it. And on that table was the biggest heap of quarters that's ever been heaped on any kitchen table, ever.

# 7

I DIDN'T BOTHER to knock. I guess my subconscious, which was the only part of my mind that was working, decided crooks didn't deserve the politeness of knocking. In I barged.

"Truman, you beat all, you know that? You throw away a perfectly—"

Truman yelped and threw himself backward so hard his chair fell clear over and he cracked his head on the floor, and Harlan howled like a turpentined dog and flung himself atop the pile of quarters, hugging them up in his arms and looking at me half terrified and half mad, that greasy stringy hair of his falling down across his eyes like black baling twine.

"How in hell did you get here?" Truman bellowed as he commenced thrashing around on the floor, trying to collect his arms and legs.

I gave him a hand. "Followed my womanly intuition. Truman, you beat all, you know that? You don't have the brains God gave a chicken, ripping off change machines."

"How much does she know? How much does she know?" Harlan yipped.

"Oh, shut up, Harlan. I'm not interested in you. It's Truman I came looking for."

With Truman upended and dusted off, I couldn't help looking at that mountain of quarters again. "How much did you get?"

I couldn't believe I'd said that. Just as though I was in on it with them. Callie Kiffin, gun moll. But at least the question relaxed Harlan and Truman, and first thing I knew we were sitting around the table, the three of us. Like partners.

"We haven't got it counted yet," Truman said, "but we're guessing a couple hundred anyway."

"Thirty-seven dollars," I said flatly. "At least according to Sedge Critz."

"Who the hell is Sedge Critz?" Truman demanded.

"Runs the drugstore."

Harlan said, "Truman, get your girl friend out of here. This ain't none of her business."

"It is now." I gave him a straight look.

He scrunched down into his shoulders and said, "What you going to do, turn us in?"

I debated.

"Nah, she won't," Truman murmured, running his hand around the back of my neck. "Callie's my buddy, aren't you, darlin'? She's on my side."

"I was on your side when you were a bum, and when you were a ranch hand. But this," I waved toward the heap of silver, "I don't know about this, Truman. This is a whole other ball game."

78

"You gonna turn us in?" Harlan demanded.

"How should I know, Harlan?" I yelled. "I just now walked into this mess and found out my supposed boyfriend is a cheap crook. I haven't had time to figure out what I'm going to do about it. Just butt out, will you?"

"Harlan," Truman said with quiet dignity, "would you please excuse us for a minute? Callie and me have to talk."

"Sure," Harlan said, but he didn't move, just sat there looking from Truman to me.

I said, "Harlan, leave."

"Oh. I thought you meant *you* were going to leave." He got up and went outside, muttering, "It's my house, after all."

I looked at Truman. "What are you doing hanging out with an empty bucket like him?" I said in a controlled voice.

Truman shrugged and started playing with the quarters, trying to make them stand on edge.

"Okay then, if that was too tough a question, tell me what happened with the ranch job."

He shrugged again. "I don't know. It was hot out there, Callie. That Coop, he had me building feed bunkers out in that hot sun all day. It was giving me a dizzy headache. I wanted to run into town to get us a six-pack of beer, and Coop wouldn't let me. I'm not used to having to ask somebody's permission for a thing like that, Cal. I'm my own man. I don't belong to that turkey."

"You do if you're working for him."

"That's why I ain't working for him any longer."

"But Truman, what do you intend to *do* with your life? You've got to work for somebody, and it's always going to be the same thing, people giving you orders. You might just as well get used to it."

The obvious answer hung in the air between us but I ignored it and talked faster. "Listen, Tru, so okay, you don't want to work for anybody else. Then get into some profession where you can be your own boss, like I'm doing. There's got to be something you'd enjoy doing, where you could be your . . . own. . . ."

The obvious answer popped up between us again.

Truman grinned down at the heap of quarters.

"Aw, no, Truman, come on. Join the real world. You can't make a career out of. . . ." I motioned to the quarters.

He grabbed my hand and looked me in the eye, and I knew he was talking straight. "Listen, Callie. Just think about it for a minute. Now Harlan and I put in maybe six hours of work last night. More play than work actually. We broke into some office machine store in Fort Supply, ran off two hundred fake dollar bills on their photocopier, cut them to size on their paper cutter, made the rounds of four car wash places and cleaned out their change machines. It was so easy! The cops could have driven right past and never known we weren't just in there washing our car. The whole thing was fun, and we ended up with a hundred bucks apiece, pure profit, and tax free. Now you got to admit that beats being somebody's slave all week in the hot sun."

80

"But it's stealing!"

"Of course."

"But Truman, that money belongs to somebody."

"Sure. Me and Harlan. Unless you're going to want a cut for not turning us in."

"Truman," I snapped, and hit him on the arm, "knock that off. Come on now, doesn't it bother you that you were taking money that rightfully belongs to the people that own those car washes? Maybe they're just scraping by themselves and need every penny they can earn."

"Nah, if they own car washes, they've got all they need."

It's surprising how hard he was to argue with, even when I knew he was dead wrong. I sat back in the chair and stared at him. "So you're going to make a career out of this, are you?"

"Might for a while anyway, till I figure out something better."

"Uh-uh. I see. You and Harlan, right?"

"For now anyway. He's the one who knows these towns around here. He knows where stuff is. And he's got this place. Course, I'll be getting a place of my own as soon as I've got the money."

That raised another question. "What about Doc and your mom? What are you going to tell them, that you're still working at John's ranch?"

"No, I thought I'd tell them I've got a night job, truck driving or some such where they can't check up on me and where the hours would be flexible. You're not going to tell them any different, are you, darlin'?"

I gave him a dirty look, but I knew and he knew I

81

wasn't going to rat on him. "I was over there last night, looking for you. I think I dropped a hint that you weren't working at John's ranch."

"That's okay. I'll just tell them I tried it for a week and then got this better job."

Being an accomplice felt lousy. Right then I wanted nothing more to do with Truman Johnson and company, especially since he obviously didn't need me any longer, now that he had Harlan. I got up and started toward the door, but all of a sudden he was blocking my way, looking down at me with that warm, loving look. He wrapped his arms around me and pulled me in close and kissed me. A lot.

"That's not going to do you any good," I muttered. "I already told you I wouldn't tell."

"Callie."

"What?"

"You're beautiful."

I laughed. "Oh, come on. Tell me another one."

"You are. To me, you are. You're so tiny and petite."

I loved that. Petite sounds so much better than scrawny.

"And yet you're so strong," he went on, whispering. "You're a lot better person than me, and don't think I don't know that. I just wish I could be like you."

"Well, you can, fool. What do you think I'm trying to help you do? But you're not exactly cooperating, you know. It's like pushing a chain uphill, trying to make something out of you."

He grinned and chuckled and kissed the end of my nose. Mad as I was at him, I really liked that little kiss on the end of my nose.

"Just for the sake of curiosity, Truman, how did you figure out about photocopying dollar bills and all that? I assume you're the brains of the outfit."

He rubbed his cheek against my hair and said softly, "That Tumbleweed Ranch was a very educational place. There were guys there that had pulled some fantastic things. Hell, I was considered the dull kid on the block, just selling grass. Sometime I'll tell you—"

"I don't want to hear about it, okay? Listen, I said I won't tell anybody, and I won't, but I don't want to get dragged into stuff like this. I don't want to throw away my reputation."

"I can understand that. But you're still my girl, right? I mean, nobody knows what I'm doing, and nobody's going to know, not if I'm careful and smart. So we can go out together, nights when I don't have to drive a truck, right?"

I sighed. He was hopeless. "Truman, I think a lot of you, you know that. And for a while there I thought maybe I could be a good influence on you. But it doesn't look like you're in the market for a good influence, and California Kiffin doesn't hang out with crooks."

He rared back and looked at me with such beseeching eyes that I weakened just a hair. "Callie, don't leave me. I need you. More than you know. You're the only good thing I've ever had in my life."

That was probably true.

"I'll tell you something I never told anybody before, Callie." His voice was low and intimate. "I'm no psychologist or nothing like that, but I suspect that the reason I do things like," he waved toward the quarters, "is be-

83

cause I have such low self-esteem. I don't figure anybody good would ever like me, much less love me, so I hook up with people like Harlan just so I won't be alone in the world."

There was a flaw in there somewhere. "You've got a perfectly good mother. And Doc."

"Yeah, but they don't count."

I almost knew what he meant. Winning the love of somebody besides your parents, that's where you succeed or fail, and the whole world is watching to see which it's going to be.

He was hanging onto me with his eyes and I was suddenly convinced that he did honest-to-God need me. He was actually scared I was going to drop him. That made me feel so good!

I pulled his head down and gave him a soft kiss. "Don't worry, I'll be on your side as long as you want me to be."

I went out the door and into sunlight so bright it made my eyes tear and I almost ran into Harlan.

"You gonna turn us in?" he whined.

"Oh, go sink a derrick on your head and get rich," I muttered, and drove out of there.

Talk about mixed feelings. All the way back to town I tried to sort myself out, and all I ended up with was how tremendous it felt to have someone need me as much as Truman did. Not need of my body; that would be easy enough to get, even with a barbed-wire figure like mine. All I'd have to do is flash it around a little. I knew that. But that wouldn't be worth anything. Not like having someone need my . . . essence. My inner self, whatever you want to call it. The good qualities that I knew I had

84

even if the guys at school had never noticed. Integrity and personal strength and honesty and all that stuff, well, nobody but Pop had ever valued me for those things before.

Gee, it felt good.

And I told myself, if I pretended I didn't know what he and Harlan were doing, what could it hurt? It was only temporary anyhow, until my influence started to outweigh Harlan's.

You think that my life would be all up in a heaval after that, wouldn't you, with my boyfriend turning into a cheap crook instead of the steady rancher I had him planned out to be. But the funny thing was, the days and weeks just sort of slid past, like they do in summer and it all got to be sort of everyday, you know? I was working my tail off for Doc, or rather for that paycheck, five and a half days a week, going out with Truman Friday and Saturday nights and maybe once or twice during the week, just like regular people. Mom thought it was nice I finally had a boyfriend. Pop didn't say much.

Doc was taking me with him on the ranch calls more and more often, leaving Yvonne to take phone calls in the office. First thing I knew, I was doing the driving while Doc laid his head back and napped between calls. Good practice for me, driving a pickup, he said. Sure, but how much practice does it take, I ask you? I also seemed to be doing more than half of the chasing cows around corrals and into pens, sitting on their heads while Doc did things to their other ends, and so on. I never complained. I was getting paid, and that was the main thing. But I knew, and Doc knew, he was getting a whole

85

lot of mileage out of me beyond what he'd told me the job was going to be.

I did finally stand up on my hind legs and tell him that if he was going to work me like a field hand he'd better start feeding me like one, and the lunches got better.

Along about the end of June, Truman moved out to Harlan's place. He didn't say much to me about it, only that his mom and Doc were driving him up the wall, always asking questions about his job and treating him like a kid.

And Doc didn't say much about it except to look relieved. I think Yvonne felt bad, but then I tried to avoid her whenever possible on account of how she sprayed when she talked, so I never really knew how she felt.

I was leery of the whole idea. It was hard to think of Harlan as dangerous. He didn't have two brains to rub together and as far as I could see, the main thing Harlan was, was lazy. But Truman's moving out there with him made me feel as though I was losing whatever headway I might have been making with Truman. Not that he asked my opinion about the move. He just did it and told me later, when he started showing up in Harlan's car instead of Yvonne's.

The funny thing was, when we went out all those nights, Truman didn't seem like a crook. Mostly we didn't talk about what he'd been doing, although I assumed he was doing something of an illegal nature since he always seemed to have money to spend. I never asked, and he never told. He was sweet and funny and loving, and we had good times. I'm not kidding you, we really began to get close.

When I thought the mood was right, I'd say something about his future—you know, going to a trade school or something like that. But it never took. One night he said, "You know, Callie, there are people in this world that just don't fit into the category of your everyday guy. I'm one of those. I think we may as well accept that fact, don't you? I mean, I'm not ever going to fit into a white collar, nor even a blue one."

"How about black-and-white stripes?" I said drily.

"Well now, that all depends on your frame of mind."

I sat up straighter—we were parked between the ball diamond and the river—and said, "You want to run that by me again?"

He took my hand and explained. "Okay, this is the way I see it. A guy can make a perfectly good living doing . . . what I'm doing now which I know you don't want to know about so I won't tell you . . . but it's just a whole hell of a lot easier than any kind of job that's ever been invented. And if you go at it with the idea that from time to time you're going to get caught and spend a few months in the county birdcage, well, it's just not all that much of a price to pay. I mean, I've known guys that have been in those places. It's no life of luxury, but it's not all that bad, and if you end up in the state pen, hell, they've got libraries and ball teams and work release programs. It's just not all that uncomfortable a way to spend an occasional stretch of time."

"You mean you actually wouldn't *mind* being in *jail*?" I pulled back from him.

"Not when you consider that it's just part of the line of work you're in. Not when you stop to think that all

87

the rest of the time you're living high on the hog, sleeping late every morning while those poor working stiffs out there are slaving away for a little bit of nothing. When you add it all up, it's an easy life, darlin'. And fun. It's a challenge, you know? Thinking up different ways of . . . you know."

"Ripping people off."

"Not people," he said staunchly. "I'd never do anything to hurt people. You know me better than that. But coin machines, that doesn't hurt anybody. Gas stations, laundromats, who does that hurt?"

I stared at him and sighed all the way up from my toenails. "I haven't made a dent in you, have I? All this time we've spent together, and the things I believe in still haven't made a dent in you."

"Aw, come here. There, that's better, that's my girl. You know how important you are to me, don't you? You're the one decent thing in—"

"Your life. I know. You keep saying that."

"It's true."

"It's your own stupid fault."

"I know it. I'm nowhere near good enough for you."

He could be so damn humble. And somehow that's how our serious conversations always ended up. Tie score.

# 8

LIBERTY MAKES A BIG DEAL out of Fourth of July, I guess because the town's name fits in so well for slogans. This year it was going to be on Monday, so the thing expanded into a three-day weekend. Midnight showings of X-rated movies Friday and Saturday nights, boat races, horse show and rodeo, street dance Sunday night, and of course your ever-popular Fourth of July parade and fireworks on Monday.

I hadn't heard from Truman all week, but I figured we'd be going to at least some of the doings over the weekend. Tell you the truth, I was kind of excited about it. I know that sounds childish, but what the heck. I'd been growing up just a skootch faster than I was comfortable with, that last month or so, and the thought of simple pleasures was kind of nice for a change.

Saturday morning, which I had off for the holiday, while I was waiting around for Truman to check in with me Don called. He was heading up to Trinkles' to do their ponies; did I want to come along and give him a hand? I wavered for a few seconds, knowing Trinkles' ponies would be an all-day job and Truman might have plans. But I couldn't resist a chance to help with Trinkles' ponies. I told Don to come ahead.

The Trinkles are these two little fat people, sort of Mr. and Mrs. Santa Claus types, so cute you just want to hug them. Twenty years ago or so they started in buying a pony here and a pony there for their grandkids to play with, and first thing you know they had a couple dozen head of fat, shaggy little Shetlands and I don't know how many donkeys. By now they had a miniature chuck wagon, covered wagon, surrey with fringe, and a scaled-down stagecoach, all pony sized, and a beautiful hitch of six matched sorrel ponies with creamy white manes and tails, black harness with jingle bells—the whole bit. They drove them in parades and did all kinds of fund-raising things with them, mostly for the Shriners' hospital that treats burned children.

When I was a little kid, Pop used to take me out there sometimes on a Sunday afternoon and I'd ride one pony after another around that big shady yard while Pop and the Trinkles sat on the porch and watched. And I went out one other time with Don to help him trim feet and reset shoes for the six ponies that did the parades. It was about the most fun I'd ever had. They had one little Sicilian donkey that runs loose around the place. It's about as big as, say, an Airedale, just a little bit of a guy. But ornery? He'd come up behind you and grab anything he saw sticking out of a pocket and run off with it. A couple of times he bit me on the hip trying to pick my pocket— but not hard enough to hurt—and those big brown eyes looking up at you under that curly mop on his forehead— well, you couldn't stay mad very long. Once he ran off

with Don's angle gauge and dropped it in the weeds somewhere and we never did find it. I was the only one who
thought that was cute.

I hung up and went outside to wait for Don. Pop was
out there in his bare feet with his pants rolled up, washing
Mom's car. You don't wash a car in Liberty, Oklahoma,
with any hopes of it staying clean, mind you, just in hopes
of minimizing the paint erosion from the alkaline dust.

If I ever got me a pickup truck, every Sunday morning
was going to be truck-washing time. And for cleaning out
the inside. No truck of mine was ever going to be the
rolling trash can Doc's was, candy wrappers and drink cans
and crud a foot deep on the floor of the passenger's seat.

I'd just started yelling in Pop's ear that I was going out
to Trinkles' with Don to get the ponies ready for the
parade, when a strange car pulled up out front and
honked. I squinted at it and bent down to see the face
inside. It looked like Truman, but. . . .

It was one of those sports cars that you get into like
putting on a boot: bright red, chrome enough to choke a
horse, and just a little bit of a cockpit for seats. The roof
was like a little bubble with windows.

Pop turned off the hose and we both stared. It was
Truman.

"Oh, my God," I whispered.

He was grinning like an idiot and waving me over.
"Cal, come take a ride."

I went over and started to lean my hands on it, to talk
down at him.

"Don't touch the paint," he snapped, then smiled again
and muttered, "Hop in quick, take a ride. I'll tell you all

91

about it." He waved and gave Pop this stupid smile and motioned me in.

I hesitated. Don was going to be . . . oh rats, there he came now. Don's truck pulled up behind the red car and he leaned over and opened the passenger door for me.

As much as I wanted to go shoe Trinkles' ponies with Don, I knew I better not go off and leave Truman sitting there grinning in the middle of more trouble than he knew what to do with.

"Hey, Don."

"Hop in, kiddo, we got a big day's work waiting for us."

"I can't go. Something just came up."

Don looked from me to Truman and the sports car and back to me again, and I could see his face change from open friendliness to suspicion, to borderline ticked-off.

"Get a better offer, did you?"

"No, it's not that. I've just got to straighten something out. It just came up."

"Uh-uh."

"I'll have him run me out to Trinkles' as soon as I've had a chance to talk to him, okay? We'll probably be right behind you. You won't even have time to get your forge fired up."

He gave me a long look. "I had planned to show you how to pull shoes today," he said, kind of heavy, and I knew he didn't believe I'd show up. "I figured those ponies would be ideal for you to learn on, and it'd be a big help to me. Twenty-four shoes to pull, and reset, that's going to be a two-man job, Cal. I figured I could count on you."

92

I felt rotten. "You can. I'll be there. Just as soon as I can. Okay? Honest."

He looked deeply dubious, shot another unloving look toward Truman, and wheeled away.

On my way to get in with Truman I glanced over at Pop. He was standing in the same spot, bare feet splayed out, pants rolled up, and garden hose flopping in his hand. He was looking at me, just looking. All of a sudden I was mad at him. Don't ask me why. I was just mad at Pop standing there passing judgment on something he didn't know anything about.

I squeezed into the little red corset, slammed the door, and said, "Let's get out of here. Get it out of town. North. You have to take me out to where Don's working so I can help him. You stole it, didn't you? Boy, you are one walking brain, you know that?"

"Not anymore," he crowed. "Not walking anymore. Driving. In style. Well? Aren't you going to tell me how you like her?"

"Are you crazy, Truman?"

"What? What do you mean? I thought you'd like it."

"You're stealing cars now, right? You've graduated from . . . whatever else you were doing and you're now in the big leagues. That's wonderful."

He looked mildly hurt by my attitude. Tough.

"Guess how much it's worth?" he said, like a little kid.

I leaned my elbow on the window and held my forehead in my hand.

"Go on, Cal, guess how much it's worth?"

"Ten years to life?"

93

"Thirty thousand dollars."

"Uh-uh. And you're going to take it down to Smilin' Sam's Used Car Lot and cash it in for thirty thousand dollars."

"No, we're taking it over to Amarillo Monday, to a guy Harlan knows. He'll take it apart, file off the numbers, and resell the parts. There's a big market for that kind of stuff. Harlan and me figure to clear five, six thousand apiece, easy."

Right then I began to know I'd lost him. No way was my good influence any match for six thousand dollars of easy money. But I was damned if I was going to give up that easy.

"Truman, didn't it ever occur to you that driving this car around town, in broad daylight, on a holiday weekend, might not be the smartest thing you ever did? I mean, this is not exactly your everyday Ford sedan, is it?"

"Oh, don't worry about that." He gave me this knowing smile. "We got it in Wichita, and it was a different color. Me and Harlan painted it ourselves in his barn last night. And it's got different plates. Nobody's going to be looking for it around here. Me and Harlan decided we'd have some fun with it this weekend, before it goes to heaven. I get it till noon tomorrow and he gets it through Monday."

I groaned. For a while we drove without talking, up one back road and down another, till it occurred to me that I was riding in a stolen thirty-thousand-dollar car and if a Highway Patrol car should come into view over the next hill, I might have my tail in the fan along with Truman's.

94

"Turn right at the next road," I told him. "I've got to get up to Trinkles'."

When we got there, Truman didn't pull all the way in. He just pulled up by the mailbox and sat there with his hands gripping the wheel and an unhappy look on his face. It struck me that he was probably scared. If he had any sense at all, he was.

"I guess you're mad at me," he said.

"I've got no right to be mad or not mad. What you do is your own business. Disappointed, I guess you could say. For a while there I had hopes that you were going to outgrow this junk and get yourself straightened out. You kept talking like that was what you really wanted, deep down. I mean, you kept saying stuff like you didn't want me to leave you because I was the only decent thing in your life. Well, it looks to me like decent just is not what you want. So if that's the case, I'm cutting loose from you, Truman."

He snapped around at me. "Aw, no, Callie. Don't say that. Don't leave me."

"Why not? I've got no intention of having anything to do with car thieves. If that's the kind of person you choose to be, then you'll have to be it without me. So don't darken my door again." I was trying for a kidding note with that last, but it didn't come off.

Do you know how hard it is to climb out of one of those little buggers, especially when your hands are shaking and you can't see very well? I stumbled and fumbled and finally got out and away.

Don didn't say much to me while we worked, just

showed me how to knock off the nail clinches and pry the shoes off with the nippers. But I was shook and he knew it and was gentle toward me.

Pop was waiting for me when I got home. It was ten minutes till time to start the first movie, so I knew he was going to be late getting to work for probably the first time in his life. That made me realize how important this was to him.

He jumped right into it as soon as I came out of the bathroom after I'd washed the main dust and sweat off my face and arms.

"I don't like what I saw you doing this afternoon," he said.

"What?"

"You know what. Promising Don you'd help him and then going off with that boy, in that car."

"Pop, I did help Don. What'd you think I've been doing all afternoon?"

I didn't like the answer I saw on his face. It was the first time I could remember Pop ever disliking me or accusing me, and it made me sick at my stomach. But mad, too. Heck, if he couldn't be depended on to be on my side, then who could?

"Callie," he said in a quiet voice, "I don't like you going around with Truman. I don't trust him and I'm scared for you."

I didn't say anything.

"Where did he get that car?" Pop asked.

I shrugged.

"Is it his?"

"I guess."

96

"He stole it, didn't he?"

I looked miserable. "We broke up this afternoon. I'm not going to be going out with him anymore, so you can quit worrying."

He looked like sunshine breaking through the clouds. He gave me a quick hug and cheek-peck and ran off to work.

I kicked some furniture.

I was glad all this happened on a holiday weekend if it had to happen. At least there were distractions. I went to the horse show and rodeo Sunday afternoon, sat in the bleachers in the hot sun and watched the battles between man and beast in the rodeo arena, and between man, beast, and electric-eye timer in the gaming ring where the local kids ran barrel races and flag races and all that. I did some halfhearted wandering around among the parked horse trailers, thinking I should be making myself known to these future customers, but I didn't have the spirit to talk to anyone. Mostly I just shuffled around with my fingers in my jeans pockets, dodging horses' rear ends and watching where I stepped.

That night I went down to the carnival, which was set up at the other end of the fairgrounds from where the rodeo and horse show were still going on. This wasn't Shelly's carnival, but since my best friend was carny I felt at home there, talking to the people that ran the games. Since everybody there was looking for action, there were occasional guys who ran their eyes over me a time or two, and if I'd looked back at them I'm sure I could have got picked up, but I wasn't in the mood.

Truman wasn't there anywhere. I know, because I looked. Thoroughly. I guess I was having that phantom-limb syndrome, like when your leg is amputated but you swear you can still feel your toes. I could still feel Truman in the middle of my life, even though I was the one who amputated him.

Being a thinker by nature, I was studying my hurts even while I was hurting. I was a little surprised that a zero like Truman was leaving such a big hole in me by his absence. I mean, I wasn't in love with him or anything stupid like that. I more than half didn't even like him. But I loved how he had seemed to lean on me, you know? He'd always acted as if I was the most important person in his life, and now I was hurt that he let me dump him without even trying to talk me out of it.

Of course he was a dud, and I was better off without him. I don't need you to tell me that. But I missed the jerk. To be honest, I missed the kissing, too, even though when we were doing it I was usually pretending he was somebody else.

On Monday I went downtown to watch the parade. I got a mild buzz out of watching the ponies I'd helped shoe, pulling their miniature covered wagon with Mr. and Mrs. Trinkle sitting up there dressed like pioneers and waving left and right and having a ball.

Truman wasn't at the parade.

That night I went over to the park and watched the fireworks awhile. Truman wasn't there either.

The next morning Sedge Critz brought in his old Schnauzer, who had been passing blood in his urine over the weekend.

"Say," he said, "you hear about Harlan Wilke? Got arrested last night, possession of a stolen vehicle. Some fancy sports car. That Harlan never did have a lick of sense."

You know how they say your blood turned to ice water? That's exactly how I felt. I was standing hunched over my desk writing up Sedge's bill, and I just sort of froze there.

Doc, who still had Fritzie Critz under his arm, said, "They arrested him, did they? Got him in jail?"

I wondered then if he had his suspicions about Truman. But neither Doc nor I asked whether anybody else had been arrested with Harlan. Didn't want to give away what we were thinking, I reckon. And we knew if there was any more to the story Sedge would have told it, especially if Doc's stepson was any way involved.

That night I was so full of restless energy I couldn't sit still. Pop went to work and it gradually got darker, and the darker it got the antsier I got. I knew Truman was going to show up. I didn't turn on the house lights, just the television in the living room, and I had the sound turned down way low.

It was almost ten when I saw him skulking around in the trees out by the sidewalk. I waved him in and he came.

"Your folks home?" he whispered.

"No, the coast is clear, you stupid fugitive. Come on in."

We sat in the living room and talked by the white light of the TV screen. It made Truman look sick, which he probably was. I've never seen anybody so scared. He told me all about it, how Harlan had the car out, just driving around the back roads having fun with it. Only

99

he hadn't come home, and around midnight or a little after, a cop car had come cruising up the road. Truman had seen it coming and skinned out the bedroom window and hid in the wheat field while the cops went through the house and barn and sheds. He knew they had Harlan and were probably looking to see if Harlan had been in it alone.

"Did you leave anything in the house of yours that could be identified?" I hissed.

"No, course not. A few clothes, but they wouldn't be able to tell mine from Harlan's. We're both the same size, or near enough. There's no way they could tell two guys were living there."

"Not from the housecleaning, that's for sure."

"Callie, darlin', I'm in trouble. Now I know you said you were through with me, and I don't blame you. I'm as good-for-nothin' as they come."

"*Now* you get honest."

"But you're the only friend I've got. You're the only true friend I ever had. If you don't help me now, I don't know what I'll do."

I sighed. "What is it you need?"

"Money. A place to stay. I can't go back to Harlan's. They'll be watching the place. I spent all day hid out in that wheat field waiting for dark so I could come to you. And then I had to walk all the way into town, and I haven't had anything to eat since last night."

I sighed again and gave him the dirtiest look I could, but it's hard to hate a man that hasn't eaten in twenty-four hours. Without turning on any lights, we went into the kitchen. He wolfed down sandwiches as fast as I could

100

make them, and we filled a paper bag with more sand-wiches, apples, and cans of pop. There was fifteen dollars in Mom's grocery fund in the drawer under the telephone, and I had eighteen in my billfold that was supposed to last me all month for spending money. I was allowing myself twenty-five a month out of my paychecks for walking-around money. Not without serious pangs, I folded those bills and jammed them into Truman's shirt pocket.

"Thirty-three dollars isn't going to take me very far," he muttered.

"Tough toenails. This is your chosen profession, buster. You could have had a nice, honest job building feed bunkers—"

"Okay, okay. Listen, I better get going. I'm going to hitchhike to Fort Supply and try to get set up over there somehow. I'll keep in touch and let you know where I am, so I can pay you back this money. Thanks, Callie. I knew I could count on you. I love you. Don't tell anybody I was here."

And with one swift kiss, my Prince Charming dis-appeared into the night.

# 9

I THINK Pop guessed what had happened that night, even though I went to the bank the next day and withdrew enough to replace the fifteen dollars in the grocery fund and bought a loaf of bread to camouflage the damage Truman had done to our food supply. He watched me a lot those next few days, and once or twice he asked questions that would have opened the subject if I'd been willing to talk.

But I wasn't. I didn't know for sure that Pop wouldn't turn Truman in to the police for the sake of keeping me safe from him, and I didn't want to take that chance. Not that I hadn't been tempted to turn him in myself a time or two, for his own good or for revenge because he had chosen Harlan over me. Or Harlan's life-style over mine. Whatever. But I knew I couldn't do that to Truman. That'd be like getting a rabbit to trust you and then making stew out of him.

Something between Pop and me had been damaged, and I didn't know if it was ever going to heal over. There were things in my life that I couldn't tell him, and every time I had to lie to him—even little lies of evasion—it made me feel sour about myself and sour toward Pop for putting me in that position, even though none of it was his fault.

For the first time I was beginning to understand how Mom had felt all these years, having Pop loving and forgiving her and wanting to do for her, even though she didn't deserve it and they both knew it. That sort of indebtedness could make you hate a person after a while and hate yourself for not being as good as he was.

July went by slowly. I was in a bad mood most of the month. August wasn't starting out much better. And then one morning Doc came into the office looking like a bear. He'd started coming in later and later, leaving it to me to tell people he was out on an early-morning emergency call and I'd let them know when he was available.

"My, you're looking like a ray of sunshine this morning," I said to him as he lumbered past me and headed for the beer supply in the vaccine refrigerator.

"Damn prodigal son showed up last night," he growled. "Looks like he's moving back in on us. Yvonne's thrilled." His tone left no doubt as to how thrilled he was.

"Truman?" I squeaked.

He looked at me as if to say, what a stupid question. But before we could get into it any further the phone rang, somebody out west of town with a horse going into azoturia, so Doc took off, leaving the place still and waiting.

He came while I was in the back room changing the newspapers in the hospital cage where a Siamese cat named Fido—don't ask me why—was trying to rip the bandages off his paws, which Doc had declawed yesterday. A nice, profitable, unnecessary operation, sixty bucks' worth. I

103

was explaining to the cat how he'd better stay in the house after this because his tree-climbing equipment wasn't there anymore, when I turned around and there was Truman, big as life, leaning in the doorway.

He'd shaved off his beard.

"Where'd you blow in from?" I asked, reminding myself that he was no part of my life anymore.

"Callie, aren't you glad to see me?"

"Depends on the circumstances. What are you doing back here?"

"I missed you." He came over and commenced to hug me, which isn't easy to do to a girl who's got an armload of wet cat-cage papers. "It was awful over there in Fort, Cal. I finally just gave it up and came on home. Nothing worked over there. It was always Harlan that jimmied the locks on stuff, doors and coin machines and like that. I couldn't do a damn thing without him."

"Ran out of money, in other words." I got loose from his arms and went back to the cat cage.

"It was more than that. I had lots of time to think, and I finally come to decide you were right, Callie. I want to try it your way now. Will you help me?"

"What? Go begging jobs for you, loan you money? What?"

He pulled himself up straight, and for a second there he looked the way I used to dream about him looking— you know, straight.

"No, just be my friend. Will you? I need you, Callie."

"What about Harlan?"

He shrugged. "He's still over at Fort in the county jail, waiting trial. I haven't seen him. I'm shut of him now."

104

I pondered that, wondering why Harlan hadn't named Truman as his partner. I had no faith in the idea of honor among thieves, and I sure as heck had no faith in Harlan. The only thing I could think of was that he wanted to have Truman owing him when he got out.

"I don't blame you for not trusting me after all that's happened," Truman said, "but I'm telling you this. I'm going out right today and see if Coop will hire me back, and if not I'll keep asking around till I come up with some kind of job. And when I do, then I'll feel like I deserve to have you back as my girl. Okay?"

What could I say? He was so damn humble.

Coop wouldn't hire him back. He chased him off the place, the way Truman told it, but before the end of the week Truman was working at the Chevron station four nights a week. Harlan's old job probably. It wasn't much, but it was a start. It gave him enough legitimacy to start taking me out again, and Pop couldn't say much.

Couldn't say much, but he was thinking it. I could see it in the way his eyes followed me when he thought I wasn't looking. He was worried about me and scared to say anything to me for fear of stirring up the bad feelings between us again.

Actually, after Truman started working at the station we didn't go out all that much. Sometimes he stopped in on his way home from work, at eleven, and we'd talk, and he'd kiss me, and he'd usually tell me he loved me, but things weren't wholehearted between us the way they should have been. It was as if his mind was somewhere else, and I didn't care enough to go after it.

As a reformee Truman had been interesting. Challenging. But as a steady boyfriend I've got to tell you he left a good bit to be desired: mostly smarts, and sensitivity. He just underwhelmed me with how thoughtful he could be about little things. Like the thirty-three dollars he never did offer to pay back.

But still he was a source of some pride when I compared him to how he'd been back when he was living with Harlan and ripping off vending machines or whatever he was doing for a living then.

My birthday was August eighteenth. Pop said Happy Birthday at breakfast but didn't make a big deal out of it. When I got home from work, expecting cake and presents after supper, all I found was a note saying he'd ridden into Fort Supply with Mom and he'd be home by seven or eight.

First I was frosted that he went off on my birthday night. Then I couldn't figure out how he was going to get home from Fort without a car.

Then it hit me.

I was standing in the front yard watching up the road when that metallic-blue pickup truck came into sight, and I was hugging it almost before Pop had a chance to stop it in the driveway. I hollered and danced a polka with Pop around the front yard and hugged that little man like he probably hadn't been hugged his whole life.

"How did you afford it?" I finally asked him when I could talk. We were sitting in the truck by then, and I was rubbing the steering wheel, the dashboard, the seat covers.

"I just made the down payment is all," he said in a warning tone. "Six hundred was all I could scrape to-

106

gether, so you and I will have to work together to make the payments, but I figured we could swing it. It's registered in my name because the insurance is cheaper that way, but it's your truck, darlin'. For your business."

We looked at each other for a long time, and I could see in his eyes he was saying something else to me.

"Is this some kind of a deal, Pop? Like, I get the truck if I quit seeing Truman?"

"No, hon. It's your birthday present and it's got no strings attached. Except the payments."

"But it has to do with Truman, doesn't it?"

He looked away, out the window. "You know I never liked that boy, nor trusted him. The fact that he's working in a gas station instead of . . . whatever it was he was doing for a living before"—and his look told me he knew—"doesn't make him good enough for you. I'm not trying to buy you off him. I don't want you ever to think I'd try to do something like that. All I'm hoping is, this truck might get your mind more back to where it was before. Planning for your future. You used to read me those pamphlets from the farriery schools, and those equipment catalogs, and we'd sit around planning how much it was going to cost to get you outfitted—"

His voice kind of broke there, like he was reminiscing about something wonderful. That shook me up, to think that sharing my dreams had meant that much to him.

I gave him a hug and a smack and said, "Well, we all have our price. I guess mine is a used pickup truck. Just kidding. Don't look at me in that tone of voice. And anyway, I was getting tired of Truman. He's not among the great minds of the western world."

We went for a drive all over town, and when it came time to feed the truck, I deliberately went to the Esso station instead of the Chevron.

Of course I began driving to work, just so I could look out the front window during the day and feast my eyes on my truck. It was like looking at my future, and it was so exciting that I didn't have much room left in my head for Truman. It was several days before I realized that he hadn't been over lately.

Then one night he did show up, and it wasn't after work, it was instead of work.

"Fired," I said.

He nodded and looked miserable. "They said I was coming in late too much and I wasn't fast enough getting out on the drive when customers came in. I guess I'm just not much good after all."

I was inclined to agree, but he looked so down that I ended up spending the evening with his head in my lap, stroking his hair and trying to think up positive things to tell him about himself. After a while he got to feeling better, and that made me feel good, like I still had some power over him. When he left I walked out with him to show him my truck, and he offered to check it out for me under the hood some time. He said he'd learned a lot about auto mechanics working at the station.

The next day he came into the office and got the truck keys and drove off in it and brought it back a couple of hours later with an oil change and three new spark plugs. I began to think maybe he wasn't totally worthless after all.

\*　　\*　　\*

I dreamed someone was pounding on a door. Dream melted into black bedroom and I sat up, my heart going a mile a minute.

A light was shining up from downstairs, and I heard voices, Pop's and some man's. I rolled out of bed and met Mom in the hallway. We looked at each other, puzzled and scared.

Two uniformed policemen stood just inside the front door with Pop, who was clutching his pajama bottoms around his waist and trying to shove Adolf away from the blue pants legs with his bare foot. Mom and I ran down, asking questions faster than anyone could listen.

The one cop was saying, ". . . blue pickup with white topper. The witness was only able to get a partial license plate number, but what she got matches yours."

"What! My truck? What happened to my truck?" I bounced past the cops and looked out the door, but the truck was parked there in the driveway, all in one piece But not as close to the house as I'd left it, was it?

In answer to my jibbering the cop said, "Apparently your truck was used tonight in a break-in, an armed robbery and a shooting incident, young lady. Can you tell me where you were this evening?"

I stared at him, drop-jawed. "Armed robbery? Shooting? Who? What . . . ?"

"She was right here at home," Pop said, bristling.

"Who was shot?" I demanded. "Was it serious?"

I was getting scared. Really scared.

The cop looked down at me for a while, like he was trying to figure out how much it was safe to tell me.

109

Finally he said, "The Ace Hardware store was broken into and a handgun and ammunition were taken. Then a short time later John Gray's house was broken into. Mr. Gray surprised the burglar and took a bullet in the leg. He's been taken to the hospital. His wife looked out the window and saw your truck, or one very much like it. Is there anything you can tell us about this?"

I was numbed.

Pop said, "John Gray?".

The cop nodded. "You know him, do you?"

Pop just sort of nodded, dazed.

The cop turned his hard eyes back to me and said, "Well, young lady? You got any idea who might have done it?"

My truck. He must have had a duplicate key made yesterday while he was supposedly giving it an oil change and new spark plugs.

That damned Truman. My truck!

I looked the cop dead in the eye and said, "You better believe it."

# 10

WHAT A NIGHT that was! I don't ever want to go through anything like that again, let me tell you. I stood there spilling my guts, telling that cop everything there was to tell about Truman, and shaking so hard Pop had to hold me up.

The cops took notes, thanked me, told me to be at the station first thing in the morning to give them a formal statement, and then they left. The door closed and there was this terrible stillness in the house.

Mom finally broke it. "How could you have got mixed up with somebody like that, California? This stuff has been going on all this time, and you knew about it and never said a word to anybody. I can't believe you'd get yourself mixed up in . . . stealing. Car-thieving. And now this business with John."

Pop turned on her. "Norma, shut up."

I stared at him, and so did Mom.

"Just shut up now," he said in a more normal voice, "and go on up to bed. I'll take care of Callie."

She looked from him to me and hesitated, as though she

knew she should be doing something motherly but didn't know how and didn't really want to try.

"It's okay, Mom. I'm coming up to bed in a minute."

Then her face took on a different look and suddenly I knew she was feeling shut out of the closeness between Pop and me, and she was hurting. I started to make a move toward her, but she'd already turned and started climbing the stairs.

I felt better when she was gone. Right now I had all I could handle thinking about what Truman had done to John Gray, and what I'd just done to Truman.

Pop and I sat down on the davenport, just sat there with my hands crunched up inside his.

"You want something to eat, or drink?" he asked.

I shook my head. I couldn't have moved right then if the house had been on fire. "Do you think they're arresting him at this very minute?" I whispered.

"If they are, he brought it on himself." Pop's voice was deeper and stronger than usual.

"With a little help from his friend, the squealer."

"No, hon. None of this is your fault. You did everything a friend could be expected to do, and more. If you'd gone on shielding him after what he's done tonight, you'd have been committing a crime yourself. You'd have been dead wrong not to turn him in when you did. You can see that, can't you?"

My body was beginning to melt from rigid down to shaky. "But I didn't do it to be right, Pop. I did it because he used my truck." My voice shot up out of control in a kind of hysterical half-laugh.

"That don't matter, hon." He pulled me in and held me till the trembling eased up, and his voice had a little smile in it.

"Sure it matters. I did the right thing maybe, but I did it for the wrong reason. I wasn't thinking about upholding the law or protecting Truman from himself or anything noble like that. I was just damned mad that he'd used my truck in it. Pop, I've got to wonder whether I would have turned him in if it hadn't been for the truck."

He chuckled a little more and rubbed his hand hard up and down my arm. "It ain't all that important, Callie. Really. You go to scratching under the surface of anybody's motives, you're going to find selfish reasons for everything. That's just human nature."

"Not for you. You're the most unselfish person I know."

I expected him to say something. When he didn't, I twisted around to look at his face. It was so sad I wanted to bawl.

I wanted to explore that thought, but there was too much else going on in my head. "I wonder if John's going to be all right."

Pop shrugged.

"I feel responsible for this whole mess," I muttered. "If I hadn't got John to give Truman that job in the first place, Truman probably never would have known about John. Or maybe he did it out of some kind of grudge, because Coop wouldn't give him his job back."

"I doubt that. If Truman'd wanted that job so bad, he wouldn't have walked off it like he did."

"Pop, I tried so hard with him. I honestly thought I

113

could get him to straighten himself out. He kept telling me he loved me, and it seemed like if he really had, he would have wanted to make himself into the kind of guy I could love back. Wouldn't you think?"

Pop snorted a little blast of warm breath against my hair. "He was a losing proposition from the first on, that was all. There wasn't a thing you could have done to change him. Hon, you have to realize there's a difference between basically good people who just haven't had the breaks, and basically no-good people who are never going to amount to a hill of beans no matter what you do for them."

I sat there and pondered that. "I believe you're right. Heck, Truman had his chances. He just didn't have what it takes to use them. He made choices right along, didn't he? He chose to throw away the ranch job in favor of easy pickings with Harlan and the coin machines." My voice got stronger as my convictions got stronger. "Heck, what am I sitting here feeling guilty for? Truman was the one who decided to go out tonight and break into a hardware store and rob a home and shoot an innocent man. Whatever happens to him on account of that decision, that's his fault, not mine."

"Right."

I thought some more. "He was just using me, wasn't he, Pop?"

"I expect so."

"I mean, he'd get lonesome and want a friend, so he'd come around acting like he really cared about me and all it was was his ego needing a boost, or else he was needing money, or whatever. What a creep."

114

"Well, don't be too hard on him. Everybody uses people. Everybody needs things, hon, and the only way we can get them is from other people, and sometimes that means we have to use them. You can't condemn him too hard for that."

"I don't use people," I said in a stony voice.

"Sure you do." He said it gently. "You were getting something out of what was going on between you and Truman, just like he was. Weren't you?"

I thought about it. "I guess I was kind of enjoying the idea of . . . being a sheero." I grinned down at my lap. "I was imagining being really important in somebody's life, you know? So I guess that would qualify as a selfish motive, huh?"

He chuckled. "That don't mean it was bad. Like I said, just about everything that anybody does in this world is based on a selfish motive of some kind if you dig deep enough. But that's not so important, when you get right down to it. Just so you're not fooling yourself thinking you're the only one who's not playing that game."

For a long time we sat there thinking. After a while I said, "You know, all this time I've been blaming Mom for not treating you better than she does because I figured you did such a good thing for her—you know, marrying her and all that. But I guess when you stop to think about it, you were getting something out of the deal, too, weren't you?"

He nodded against my head.

"You got me, for whatever that's worth," I offered.

"I always wanted a family," he said in a faraway kind of voice. "When I was a young man and all my friends were

115

getting married, having kids, buying houses, I felt so left out. I used to cry sometimes, you know that? I felt like the whole world was going by me in pairs, and I was the only one that nobody wanted. It was killing me inside."

All night I hadn't cried, not for John Gray nor for Truman nor myself, but a wet one was sure sliding down my face now.

He went on. "Your mom never did love me. We both knew that. No matter what I did for her or bought for her, she was always looking over the top of my head and wishing I wasn't there. Sometimes I used to think I'd have been better off if I hadn't married her. But then when you started growing up, turning from a baby into a person, well, you made it up to me. Everything I never got from the rest of the world I was finally getting from you. So don't you ever, ever think you have to take up with somebody like Truman Johnson just for the sake of being important in somebody's life, you hear?"

I nodded and sniffed.

After I gave my statement to the police stenographer the next day at Fort Supply, I went back to the visitors' room in the rear of the jail. The guard brought Truman up and we sat at a long, yellow table and looked at each other while the guard leaned against the wall and picked at his teeth.

"I wasn't expecting you to come and see me," he said finally. He looked different. He looked like a convicted criminal, that was it. And he looked, I don't know, separated from me. As if we didn't even know each other.

116

"Are you mad at me?" I said, not caring.

He shrugged. "I guess I shouldn't have used your truck, huh?"

"Damn right. You knew how I felt about that truck."

He shrugged again, as if it didn't matter.

"Well, I guess we won't be seeing each other again," I said.

He looked away.

"You chose this, you know," I said as I stood up to leave. No point in staying.

He didn't say anything.

"You told me once that going to jail every once in a while was just the small price you'd have to pay for having such an easy life and not having to work like the rest of us. Does it still feel that way, Truman? Look at me. I'm curious. I'd really like to know. Do you still feel like you made the right decision?"

He still didn't say anything, but his jaw got hard and his eyes looked disdainful. I felt as though he'd moved way far away from me and my life, as though he was already a long way down the road he'd picked out for himself.

I walked out of there feeling as if the weight of the world was coming off my shoulders.

The only bad part was passing Doc and Yvonne in the hallway. She looked terrible. Doc just looked like himself, and he said I should get back to the office as soon as I could and move today's appointments to tomorrow. But poor old Yvonne looked as though she'd been wrung out and hung out, and I felt sorry for her.

117

My truck was impounded for evidence, so we all drove home together in Mom's car. We didn't talk much, but we felt like a family, you know?

That all happened three years ago, and I was always glad for that little time in there when we really felt like a family, because things changed after that.

First, let me put your mind at ease about John. It was a clean shot through the calf of his leg and it healed, all but a nifty little scar, which he now enjoys showing off to his friends around the pool. I see him every six weeks when I go out there to reset the shoes on his daughter's horse that the Grays keep around for sentimental reasons, even though Marilee is in art school in London. John didn't hold any grudge against me for Truman. He says you can't go from girlhood to womanhood without making an ass out of yourself over at least one no-good bum. He said it was part of the rites of passage.

I shouldn't say this for fear of bragging, but I want you to know that I wasn't beating an empty drum when I talked about going to farriery school. I graduated from the Southwest School of Farriery second in my class of eighteen, and the two other girls in the class did real well too. In fact, we got to be good friends and we still get together when we can.

This year I paid off my truck. Pop had to help a lot that first year when I was still in school, but I did what I could and as soon as I was earning, I paid him back. At first he wasn't going to take it, but I told him I didn't want him feeling like he was buying my love. He backed off then, and we settled down into a more fifty-fifty friend-

118

ship. We do things for each other, but it's more equal now, and it's because we want to.

That first year I was trying to get my business going was pretty lean. I'd get a job maybe once or twice a week, and then it got a little more frequent but it was still tight. Then Don did a wonderful thing for me. He moved away. He got in with some racehorse owners down around Tulsa, and one of them offered him a live-in job on their big fancy breeding farm, and he took it like a shot. That opened up the whole Liberty area for me, and by now I'm making a darn good living, if I do say so myself. Working my tail off, of course, but I love it.

The bad part of these last three years was that Mom divorced us and married a proctologist she knew from the hospital. It was awful hard on Pop at first, but then he bounced back and healed over so well that I had to wonder how much he really had loved her, by the time she finally cut loose from him.

The funny thing is, now Mom and I get along better than we ever did when she was living at home. She's happy now, for one thing. She's got a husband she's proud of. That thought makes me cringe inside since I feel like she should have been proud of Pop for what a good person he is. But I guess being a doctor's wife means a lot to her, so I'm glad she got what she wanted.

For a while there I was bothered by what Pop and I talked about that night, about good people doing good things, most always for selfish reasons. It seemed like such a cynical way to think about people. I knew it was true, though. The more I thought about Pop the more I could see that he'd been getting his rewards all these years, and

119

not just from having me for a kid. Somewhere down deep in him, he was getting his chance to feel equal to Mom and even superior, because he'd bailed her out when she got in trouble. Like doing things for Mrs. Hendrickson all the time. It made him feel good about himself, so all the time and work he put in over at her house wasn't really a total gift.

And Don. All the times he took me with him and taught me stuff, I'm sure he was getting a charge out of getting to play teacher and having me look up to him and all that.

And God knows my ego was having a picnic all that summer feasting on Truman, on how important I was in his life and how superior he made me feel. Of course I am superior, but that's beside the point.

What I started to say was that after I'd thought about it a while, it didn't seem cynical anymore. It was like we were all on a level, you know? The good people like Pop and John and the fairly good people like me, we're all basically selfish, but who cares? We're also unselfish. I'm glad Pop can feel good about himself by painting Mrs. Hendrickson's house trim, and I'm glad things between him and Mom aren't as unequal as I used to think they were.

I'm selfish enough to be glad Pop bought me my truck, and unselfish enough to be glad it made him feel like a big guy when he scraped together that six hundred for the down payment. So it all comes out even, and I don't have to worship the super-gods of the world anymore the way I used to. I can see now that they're playing the same game I am, just with different moves.

But I'll tell you one thing. It's a whole lot more pleasant if you can get through life with people liking you than not liking you.

Poor old Truman. He turned out just about the way you figured he would. I was over at Doc's the other day getting Adolf his distemper booster shot, which he probably didn't even need, and Doc told me Truman had just been picked up in Denver for armed robbery. He'd served sixteen months on the John Gray shooting and then got out because the prison was overcrowded. So now he's at it again, and I'm sure by this time he's a hardened criminal.

Well, tough luck. He had his chances and he made his choices. I'm just thankful I had the good sense to cut loose from him when I did. He could have really messed up my life.

When I add it all up, I'm glad he was in my life for a while. As John said, he was part of my rites of passage.

It would have been nice though, wouldn't it, if I could have been a sheero and made something out of him?

It was worth a shot.